Dark Space

Edited by
Leonie Skye

Contributions by
Yvette Franklin, David Preyde, Leslie Kung,
Colin Stricklin, Lynn Finger, Luka Dowell,
Heather Dubois

Dark Space edited by Leonie Skye

Copyright © 2017 by Elm Books

Paperback ISBN: 978-1-941614-21-1

E-Format ISBN: 978-1-941614-22-8

Print Edition

Elm Books

1175 State Highway 130

Laramie, WY 82070

(elm-books.com)

Cover photo and cover art by Sarah Meacham

(sarahsuttnermeacham.wordpress.com)

Formatting by BB eBooks

Table of Contents

Foreword   v

Rhythm of the Stars   by Yvette Franklin   1

Nanny   by David Preyde   39

Lazarus Squad   by Leslie Kung   67

Ars Kinetica   by Colin Stricklin   115

Almost Human   by Lynn Finger   153

The Fate of Sunlight   by Luka Dowell   179

The Shepherd   by Heather Dubois   199

Contributors   215

Want more from Elm Books?   219

Foreword

Since H.G. Wells's 1904 short story, "The Country of the Blind," science fiction has explored the social contexts of capability. In given circumstances, a disability can disappear, or something typically considered a strength – sight, for example – can become an obstacle.

However, despite science fiction's mission to show new worlds, few stories place a person with a disability in the lead, with all of the complex flaws, emotions, strengths, and pride of a hero. The hallmark of the seven stories in Elm Books' first science fiction anthology is precisely that disabilities don't disappear. But nor are they used as devices to provoke sympathy or highlight another character's goodness. These protagonists own their disabilities as differences that are as much a part of their identities as a facility with spaceship mechanics or radio interferometry or sleuthing. The fierce storytelling of these seven authors renders their protagonists humanly heroic as they wrestle with the darkest elements of the universe.

Travel with us to the distant moons, remote space stations, and unearthly nightmares of Elm Books' first science fiction anthology.

Leonie Skye, August 2017

Rhythm of the Stars

by Yvette Franklin

I

WHAT A DUMP, Sali thought as she walked across the Boah Transplanetary Airfield. A miserable small time, small town airfield on the most reactionary rock in the Federation, a synth planet around dim Proxima Centauri. Didn't even have an automatic traveler gate, reducing her to hoofing it across what her scanner and nose identified as tarmac, a smell she hadn't experienced since she was a small child. Only reason Boah was even in the Federation was because they wanted to be part of the Transplanetary Cricket Union. She knew it must have galled the lily white goodfolk of Boah to end their ban on immigrants, the condition for entering the Fed, but the lure of trading wickets with the real players of the game was too much. She admitted to getting a thrill every time New Trinidad or Hindia trounced them.

Her stop was completely unscheduled, but she'd just won a bid on a big sense-ship exploration mission of Luhman 16AB and needed someone with a Hands Cert pronto. Her previous

Hands had left to join his spouse on a last-minute colony mission to Eridani, where most of the action was these days. The Centauri synth planets like Boah were so 21st-century.

She could have been the Hands, having a rare triple cert in Nose, Mouth, and Hands, but she was already shipping as a Nose. Janus Hanson and Olivia Rega, her Ears and Mouth crew, were superb, spouses and a great comm tech and cook/surgeon combo. Nani Chu, her Eyes crew, was a bright young thing who'd grown up on ships and was a brilliant data analyzer. But she needed a practical type who could lug around space bales and wield a monkey wrench on her aging Comet LG-16. At least a backwater like Boah might have some techs trained on trade craft like Comets. She'd invited Janus, Olivia, and Nani to come to the Rendezvous with her to check out the Hands prospects, but they'd all yawned and said they'd rather catch up on their sleep after the jump. So she trudged across the field to Hangar 17 by herself.

JACKSOM NGATA THOMPSON pulled at the collar of his formal dress uniform as he milled around the hangar with his fellow Boah Transplanetary Academy graduates. He'd finished with a respectable top third degree from the BTA but despite the hype of Heermer Boldt, BTA chancellor and snake-oil salesman, it turned out that not a lot of ships ever stopped at the Boah Rendezvous. He didn't have the gilders to buy a ticket off-planet to attend one of the big events of Sol or Sirius. But as he was bored mindless by the local synth-rock work he and most of his fellow graduates ended up in, here he was again, hoping for that twinkly ticket off-planet that had led him to travel from Thompson Ranch, halfway across the planet, to attend BTA. Rumors had it that a sense-ship was looking for a Hands. He scanned the room for possible ship crew to connect with. He saw the officials from Tatooine Mining, purveyors of fine words and death sentences. Last two Botas who'd ended up with them had died in a mine crash. Two officials sporting the silver braid of colony crew were talking to a couple in a corner. Random other spacers were milling around.

He decided he might as well get something to eat. Boah Rendezvous fed any spacer in the vicinity to boost their transplanetary contact numbers. Airfield provision prices were typically outrageous, so always best to feed up when possible. Only person at the table was a short, dark, dumpy spacer in dingy space fatigues of no particular color with only two patches, an old Comet cap, sense goggles, and a surprisingly fancy pair of sense gloves. Probably tech crew on some two-bit ship. He realized with a start that the spacer was probably female. She seemed to be reaching for the dogs in blankets, so he reached for them for her.

"Here, ma'am," he said as he placed the tray in front of her.

Sali Watson laughed, and, switching to the John Wayne

module she often used with Anglic speakers, replied, "I wouldn't make a habit of calling me that, brushhopper."

Jacksom did a double take at the man's voice coming out of a small speaker necklace. Then he laughed in return. The spacer was channeling the Duke.

"I give ya my solemn word," he replied in his best bad John Wayne accent. And then, because at least he was having a conversation with a spacer, commented, "Like Comets, real reliable."

"Ya ever worked on a Comet ship?" asked Sali.

"Not a ship, but we used my great-uncle's lifter around the ranch. Had to have been 75 terrayears. Only thing that ever went down on it is the solar alternator."

"Yeah," said Sali. "We swapped out the alternator on our LG-16 for a Dyson years ago. Needed that for transmission speed."

Jacksom was just about to ask more about the LG when the warning bell rang for the seekers to get ready.

"They're playin' my song," he said, pointing to the bell.

"Later, pardner," Sali replied.

Jacksom made his way to the locker room, and the locker with the gear that he'd had to rent for the day. Total rip off, but cheaper than buying all the gear separately. The area was crowded. He'd realized at his first Rendezvous that far more people came than ever were seen by the public. He and his fellow BTA students had always watched the proceedings from the benches around the grounds, but hadn't realized that the people before them were just a fraction of the people at the Rendezvous. Experienced spacers with good records could be hired with just a health check and a private interview, might not even have to do the tech tests if their skills were well known. Newbies, like he had been his first year, could wash out in the unseen preliminaries—the health tests and endless computer trials.

He changed into the low-tech gray cotton t-shirt and pants they provided for the preliminaries, no nano-tech allowed. At least the t-shirt didn't itch like the uniform. A couple of his classmates were changing along with him, some people he recognized from other years, and a whole bunch of strangers. Some looked like they'd been around for years, others looked like they wouldn't even qualify for a driver's license. They made him feel old.

He walked to the testing rooms at the north end of the Rendezvous Center and exchanged his permanent idencard for a temporary competitor card that would track his results on all the tests. He was then funneled into a med-probe tunnel. He stepped on the slow walkway and followed the directions of the disembodied scanner voice.

"Take a deep breath now ….You may breathe now …. Put your arms above your head …. Put your arms down …. Touch your right finger to your nose …. Touch your left finger to your nose …. Read the top line of the following chart …. Read the next line ...." He hated the eye chart. His eyes didn't work well with traditional print. Letters always seemed to wave in front of his eyes. He'd long ago memorized the charts though. The lights along the tunnel blinked green except for a couple of amber lights for what were probably blood pressure and cholesterol, typical results of the Boah miner's diet of meat, fried starches, and double chocolate dairy creams.

SALI DIDN'T BOTHER crowding around the monitors in the observation room. Her sense goggles were practically useless with communal screens. She instead found a corner out of the traffic with a flat tech table and started reviewing lists of applicants. Many familiar names—Hands, other Perceivers, and general Techs that she green-lighted out of courtesy to get them past the preliminaries. Some might work for her ship, but she had reservations about all of them. Jobal Kinney was a prominent member of the Kinney consortium. Not only were there a couple of Kinney ships at the Rendezvous, but there was still bad blood between the Kinneys and the Watsons over the Xerka affair. Arrogance got in the way of common sense with the Kinneys just a little too often. Zyre Willis was good, lots of Comet experience, but her daughter had just given birth, and Sali knew Zyre wanted to ship to the Sol system to be close to her. Sali would of course make a couple of perfunctory bids on her, just to show the old boys' network that they couldn't low bid Zyre, but she wouldn't push the deal.

After reviewing spacers with first- or second-degree con-nections to her, she started surveying the rest of the pack, running her gloves over the screen, letting them translate the data into quickly digestible braille. She of course couldn't see it, but she had been told that it was slightly eerie to watch her communing with what looked like a blank screen. As her data analyzer Nani had observed, the less information other crews had about her decision-making process, the better.

A couple of names were marked with notes she'd taken at the meet and greet, mostly comments she'd made as she was sense scanning the room, such as "tall" or "strong hands." She downloaded her goggles' feed data and filtered through the conversation of the room to see if anyone had mentioned a Comet or other old-school ship. Only entry that came up was labeled "Brushhopper," the local who had handed her the dogs in blankets. She pressed the preliminary-interest button and switched to his data feed. He'd passed his physical with little problem, apart from the typical Boah bad diet effects. A balanced space-bar diet would take care of that. Graduated 33rd out of 105 from Boah Transplanetary Academy, a Hands-only minor vocational school. Not impressive. She monitored the info-stream as he went through basic tech tests. Acceptable on the math portion, good on manual dexterity, okay on the audio and 3-D portions, utterly dire on the visual-text portion. She flipped to the screen with his school records. No notation of dyslexia, but Boah was such a backwater that they might not be up on standard protocols. His total score was below the standard break point that automatically advanced candidates, but she pushed the pass button. She needed a pair of Hands, not a literary critic. She then scanned through the list and picked out other likely candidates. She had a choice, as she always did with her exploration missions. Everyone thought exploration was cool, even if few had the patience for it. Even Brushhopper had marked exploration on his preliminary forms. Then she keyed in her choice of tests. The audience would be amused by them. They always liked the oddball events, and hers were legendary in their oddness.

JACKSOM'S HEART SANK as he finished the tech tests. His eyes hadn't been working during the visual-text tests. The letters seemed to jump around, and gave him a headache even when just thinking about reading. Automatic pass was 196. He'd scraped a 199 last year and at least gotten to the general exhibition events, with at least one mining ship interested in him. Was glad he hadn't won that. Jem Tarrington had gotten that Tatooine contract and now he was dead.

Jacksom called up his result: 189. His heart sank deeper until he realized that next to it blinked PASS. Somebody wanted him to go through despite his dreadful scores. *Maybe somebody at Tatooine remembered me*, he thought, and then wondered if he was desperate enough to get off-planet to work for them.

He filed into the grand exhibition hall. The next phase was beginning.

"WELCOME TO THE 39th ANNUAL BOAH RENDEZ-VOUS" boomed the speakers. "GREETINGS TO SPACERS, HONORED GUESTS, BTA STUDENTS, AND OUR SEEK-ERS."

Jacksom was handed the red jacket that the previously unsigned always wore during the games. Milly from the year above him was there, easily remembered as she was one of the few women at BTA. She wore a blue Kinney jacket with a single patch. Most of the other people he recognized were in red jackets like his own. So much for BTA's illustrious record. He stood with his fellow redcoats on the left side of the auditorium, while a rainbow of colors with patches up and down their arms filled up the right side of the arena.

As soon as all the seekers had filed in, introductions began for the ships and crews. It was hard to tell who was who. As always, the spacers barely acknowledged their introductions. They liked to keep the seekers guessing who was who, even if the jackets they wore often gave them away. A cheer went up as they announced the Kinney ships, and a crowd in blue jackets nodded from the left of the podium. Much less enthusiastic applause for Tatooine, Gregory, NewCoal and the other mining companies.

When the speakers said, "Welcome Dr. Sali Watson, NMH, Captain of *The Blink*, Watson Consortium," the crowd went wild. Watsons were a spacer clan even older than the Kinneys and not usually found out at Boah. They were well known civil-rights activists and had boycotted Boah for years. He peered at the grandstand of dignitaries, trying to figure out which was the Watson captain. Didn't see any sign of Watson gold but was surprised to see John Wayne standing there. She must be more important than he'd first thought. The red jacket standing next to him saw the direction of his eyes.

"Yeah, sign the treaty and all the scum come in. Who wants to work for a darkie? And doesn't he know only blindies wear sense goggles these days?"

Jacksom said nothing. There were too many asshats like this guy to fight with on Boah. But it did set him wondering if John Wayne was blind. It was said that spacers tolerated even the worst defects. Parents on Boah would place their unwanted children, the crippled, blind, deaf, and retarded, or just the eighth or tenth child, in baskets at airfields for spacers to carry them off. One of his cousins had been exposed like that. Always wondered what had happened to him. He'd had a huge red birthmark covering most of the right side of his face. Ugliest thing he'd ever seen.

His Aunt Telli had objected to her son being exposed, saying he was perfectly healthy, but his grandfather had insisted. "Too many mouths to feed at the ranch for some defective to be cared for," he'd said. His aunt had driven for eight days, four days out and four back, to take the baby they'd nicknamed Strawberry to Boah Airfield rather than one of the local places. She figured he would be better treated at a real transplanetary spaceport than at the backside field that served the ranches. Despite the fact that Grandfather had forbidden the baby being named, she'd named him George David Thompson VIII after Grandfather and taken every pot of strawberry jam she'd made for the last three years as an offering. Even made him a blanket with spaceships and strawberries as a memory token. Telli never went down without a fight. Since she was his favorite aunt, Jacksom had gone with her as an extra pair of hands. He'd even slipped a wooden top into the basket so the kid would have something to play with. Thinking back on it, that trip was what had given him the space bug. Boah Airfield was the most magnificent place he'd ever seen. He was still amazed he was here even if he was probably going to wash out again. Wearing the red jacket made him feel like a spacer.

The speakers crackled. "We'll start with the traditional contests of weight-lifting exhibits, marksmanship, and low-grav acrobatics, then we have some special treats for you in store."

The crowd cheered and seekers began filing to their positions.

✦   ✦   ✦

SALI HAD SET her sense gloves to vibrate in response to crowd noise. The room felt like it was buzzing. She sent a note to Zyre Willis. "Will hire you if you want but doing expie."

"Need Sol 4 baby," Zyre texted back.

"KK, look out for Brushhopper, BTA 370033. Might have potential but BTA sucks rocks at training."

Sali felt Zyre's chuckle in response. Zyre could use a vibe transmitter with the best of them. "Will do. L8r," said Zyre, signing out.

Sali upped her bid on Zyre just to give the boys a run for their money and then surveyed the seekers. She had a ringside seat to better perceive the proceedings. She'd noted the people she was interested in and her goggles marked them in her sensing field. Zyre was to the left, efficiently going through the weight routines. She was a scrawny thing but she could pull her own weight well. Jobal Kinney had spent too many years in space and wasn't impressive. Of the regular spacers, a couple who had had mining experience did quite well. The redcoats were doing better. They were gravity kids and their muscles reflected it. She felt the crowd buzz when one of the redcoats lifted 200kg in a clean and jerk. He was a big guy but that was still an impressive number. Brushhopper was doing well with 150kg in the snatch. He got a decent weight up in a clean and jerk as well but his form stank. Sali could rarely sense details at a distance with her goggles but received outlines and movements quite clearly.

The marksmanship portion was next. *Interesting to see how Brushhopper does with his eyes,* thought Sali.

JACKSOM SIGHTED HIS target, imagined it in 3D, closed his eyes and pulled the trigger. Great Uncle Gilbert used to say, "You don't need to see the target, you just need to know where it is." Jacksom had taken the advice to heart back on the ranch, and all his experience was coming in handy now. He even got a round of applause at his still target score and managed the moving targets somehow. He glanced at his scores on his wristcalc. Above average and one flag of interest, perhaps the same entity that had passed him out of the preliminaries.

But now he was hyperscrewed. Yes, he had done low-grav aerobics at BTA, but the instructor had been way too fond of grain juice to keep the low-grav machine in good repair. Everybody had been afraid to use it because the low-grav and the safety cables were always on the edge of breaking.

The bubble was erected in the center of the stadium and seekers filed in. As the music started, an old slow Terra tune, all the seekers started moving. Last time, he'd been tapped out in the first two minutes. This time he had come prepared with handstands, a couple of basic flips, and some rock climbing moves, hoping to get past at least the first cut.

He was methodically going through his moves when he heard a voice.

"Catch me, kid," called a voice above him, a scrawny old lady with wild curly gray hair barely kept in place with a braid.

He lifted his arms and caught her easily. She then pulled herself up on his shoulders and did a neat double flip off. He grinned and mirrored her flips. When his favorite ranch tune came on, he whispered, "Follow me," and started leading her in the latest spins and turns from current ranch dances. All was made just a bit more special by their feet rarely touching the ground. The audience loved it and started clapping to the song.

He got lost in the music until he heard, "And now we are down to two!" and realized that they meant him and the old lady.

"Later, kid," she said, pushing off him and doing a couple of spectacular solo moves, leaving him in the dust.

He was tapped out shortly thereafter, but it had been the dance of his life.

OH ZYRE IS GOOD, thought Sali as she watched her flip and swirl. And Brushhopper was keeping up with her. He'd obviously had some experience with local dance forms, and she could just sense him trying out different things and playing with the low grav. Zyre made him look good but he also made Zyre look rad. Nice trick for a young man to pull off with an old lady. Zyre of course got the gold star at the end— the crowd had never seen her famous spider cartwheels before, and as usual they blew the galaxy away. Sali had had to turn the buzz down on her sense gloves for Zyre's final tricks because they were vibrating so hard.

"NOW," boomed the speakers, "THE JUNKYARD!" With that announcement, heavy lifters started moving stacks of oddly-shaped parts. Her identification feed began to have fits trying to name the random crap that was being pulled and pushed into the arena. She could feel the crowd loving it. Nothing like a backwater planet for a really good junk show. They had a hundred years of space gear out there. Sali was pleased. The junkyard had been her number one choice of tests. She wanted to know if any of these seekers could actually fix things. These days, techs did everything virtually, rarely a wrench goon in the whole bunch.

THE STADIUM LOOKED like Uncle Gilbert's salvage yard. The idea was to find and fix one of the engines on the floor with the random junk pieces lying around. At the bell, Jacksom's old lady dance partner immediately made for a Zep 1317 engine on the far side of the ring. Good choice. Straightforward specs on it and a lot of Zep junk in the room. The rest of the crowd ran to any motor they could grab, a couple pushing each other to claim a motor. He just stood and stared at the junk. He'd decided that he was going to do a Comet. Just maybe John Wayne had some pull with her Comet captain and could get him a berth on something, anything, that wasn't a mining scow. He knew Comets had to be in there. He'd seen the BTA junkyard used to supply this arena.

Homer Hanson, from the class ahead of him, flagged an engine on the left side of the arena. *Damn, that was a Comet,* he realized. He started clambering over junk piles. He was the last one without an engine. His heart pounded. He could do this, he just needed the right motor. He started looking for anything that he could fix when he spotted the distinctive shape of a Comet engine block under layers of other junk. He climbed over to the pile, flagged the engine as his, and then grabbed one of the e-hoists and started moving garbage away from it. Casing looked good from the outside.

He heard a roar, somebody had finished an engine. He looked around to see who it was and realized it was the old lady. She was obviously an old-school spacer with skills. By all the gods and spirits, he wanted that applause, that recognition of his abilities. He turned back to his engine. He finally cleared all the junk from the top of his target. The engine was basically clean and whole but had some broken seals. He couldn't see any supply of seals, but there was a good stack of thick synth fabric that he grabbed. Easy enough to cut new ones. When he lifted the engine fully clear of the junk pile, however, his heart sank. Running along the bottom was a huge crack. The damn thing would never hold pressure enough to start.

He could taste victory, he was so close, he just had to keep from panicking. *One step at a time,* said Gilbert's voice in his head. He started working on cutting his new seals as he replayed snapshots of all the junk in the arena in his mind. That crack needed welding, but the two welding rigs he'd seen had been claimed by other spacers.

Just as he finished crafting and installing the seals, he saw an old Zep F-1450 lifter. Those things had massive batteries. And by all the gods and spirits, if you had a big enough battery, you could weld. He e-lifted the motor to the Zep and then started rummaging for jumper cables, solder, and synth-rock clamps.

ZYRE NOT SURPRISINGLY finished first, but the rest of the competitors were struggling. Hard to tell what was going on. Boah had produced a stupendous amount of crap for the contest. Brushhopper was the last to claim his engine, but she was pleased to see that he'd gotten a Comet from somewhere. He must have been bright enough to figure out that perhaps she was interested in him. Like all Comet engines, it had seen better days. The diagnostics on her goggles spat out all sorts of codes, including a fatal engine crack. Brushhopper might have been better off going with something else, but all the reasonable engines seemed taken.

A round of applause rippled through the audience for Jobal finishing a Kenken. Lousy engines, but every Kinney learned how to fix one when they were ten. It was standard family issue. Then she felt a roar from the crowd. Nobody had finished, so somebody must be doing something amusing. Her goggles almost burned out as she turned toward the center of the excitement. She dialed the sensitivity down until she realized that someone, in fact Brushhopper, was spot welding with jumper cables. *Damn that's an old move*, she thought. The crowd was eating it up. Modern welding was done with discrete e-paddles, molecules moving about with hardly a spark. This was way more shiny and fun.

A couple of other competitors finished, but the crowd barely noticed. They were just cheering in time with the blasts of light from the welding. His first attempt at starting the engine failed, but he threw around some more sparks and tried again. This time the engine purred to life. She hit the bid button. The kid could be useful.

JACKSOM TOOK OFF his makeshift space helm cum welding gear and realized the crowd was roaring. In fact, they seemed to be roaring for him. His name with a FINISHED label blinked up on the board. He was seventh in time but first in some other category, perhaps creativity. Bid lights started appearing next to his name. *Holy Fathers*, he was going to get off the planet after all. Perky usherettes appeared to move him to the HIRED podium. He was actually going to have a choice in jobs.

Once he clambered up to the podium, he saw his old lady and walked to her side. "Welcome to the big leagues," she said in a low voice. "Just say 'Thank you for the offer, I appreciate it,' until you've heard what everybody has to say. They'll up their bid prices after the first round."

He nodded. He had a strange feeling of being a wildecow up for auction. He'd seen the hiring auction before. The spacers with the most bids got their offers first, leaving an ever-decreasing pot of good offers to the ones that followed behind. From his reading of the board, he'd done all right. He watched as the old lady went up for her bids. She politely thanked all for their offers the first round, and then the serious bargaining began. Tatooine Mining was the high bid the next round. So she announced she was continuing to consider their bid and rejected the other mining companies, but kept a couple of other bids alive as well. Third round somebody said something about Sol. She made a slight bow and announced, "I accept the offer of the Transpack Interplanetary Service."

Some Kinney was next, also got a bunch of mining offers and two Kinney ships. He eliminated all but the Kinney ships the first round, and accepted one of them the second round. Then, to his astonishment, Jacksom was third on the bid list.

"AND OUR OWN BOAH TRANSPLANETARY ACAD-

EMY GRADUATE, JACKSOM THOMPSOM, SHOWING THE UNIVERSE HOW IT IS DONE!" announced the speakers. "WINNER OF THE BTA BEST FINISH AWARD OF 5,000 GILDERS AND TIED WITH TOP ALL-TIME BOAH FINISHER."

Wow, he thought, barely able to parse the magnitude of what was happening. He, who had failed the preliminaries except for some hint of interest from someone, was the BTA Top Finisher. *Holy Fathers in the Heavens.*

Tatooine gave a solid bid, not as big as for the old lady but more money than he'd ever had in his life. Other mining companies followed suit. Each he thanked for their offer. Then a Kinney ship made an offer for a tech job. He was very tempted, but kept his excitement in check and thanked them as well. Then the Duke stepped up to the bidder's platform in her nondescript space fatigues. There was a confused buzz from the crowd until she made a quick gesture with her hand. In front of the whole audience, her suit turned from utterly bland beige to gleaming Watson Consortium gold. The crowd roared.

"DR. SALI WATSON, NMH, CAPTAIN OF THE BLINK, WATSON CONSORTIUM, OFFERS A HANDS POSITION ON AN EXPLORER SHIP AT 50,000 GILDERS," blasted the speakers.

The money was less than the others were offering, but Jacksom couldn't help himself. An explorer bunk with the

Duke—who turned out to be a Watson captain and not just some tech—was beyond his wildest dreams. He bowed and announced, "I accept the offer of the Watson Consortium." The crowd went absolutely wild. He moved to the side of Dr. Watson, held up her arm, and felt the waves of the noise from the audience roll over him. It was the best moment of his life.

SALI WAS RELIEVED that he'd taken her first offer. Her budget was limited, and she didn't want to end up giving him more than her seasoned crew. Nani said the suit was pretty spectacular when turned on, and perhaps it had helped. She was also amused by how the crowd reacted to Jacksom lifting her arm in an old-school boxing match victory gesture. So much fuss.

II

THE CAPTAIN UTTERED Jacksom's new least favorite words, "The holds need rebalancing." Even the hay barns back home had automated lift systems, but here on *The Blink* everything had to be moved by hand. His hands to be specific. He went down to the holds and started moving huge bales until the area scales rebalanced. At least it was low grav, but the work was still monumentally tedious. Turned out that a Hands position on a Watson Consortium Explorer Ship bore a close resemblance to a hand position back at the ranch. A lot of moving, shoving, lifting, and other grunt work. Worst of all, when he finished the manual tasks of the day, he had to spend his evening doing endless remedial tutorials, all the classes that either he'd bombed at BTA or that BTA had never even offered.

"HE STILL DOESN'T know a lick of Intergalatic Sign Language," said Nani in her usual fast-as-lightning signing. "He's been working on those tutorials for weeks and nothing seems to be sticking."

"Have you offered to give him lessons yourself?"

"Yeah, but he's such a Neanderthal. He keeps calling me ma'am, and doesn't seem to learn anything even if I repeat it."

Sali allowed herself a rueful chuckle. Nani was brilliant, but she was not patient. She had been a spacer since she was exposed at a very young age, probably because of her deafness, and had little tolerance for those who weren't steeped in spacer culture and lore. And Brushhopper not knowing IGSL was a huge problem. It was the standard language of the ship. Even she was getting tired of having to use her Anglic module. And things would only get worse when they hit the Phrenobian Belt between Centauri and Luhman, notorious for fritzing out electronics. She'd guessed he was dyslexic from his prelims, but the extent had only become clear as he flailed his way through so many of the preps and exams. While *The Blink* was adapted to her needs and suited her to a tee, the mods weren't much good for a sighted person with sight issues. A bit of voice adaptation was possible but Janus said the voice was in an Anglic accent quite different from what they used on Boah, so even that was difficult. Sali eventually had all of the voiced commands channeled through her John Wayne module because he at least understood that, but it strained the already limited processing capacity of the tutorial programs.

THEN THE LIGHTS went out. And the grav machine went on the fritz. Jacksom found himself floating off the floor. Thank the Fathers and Spirits that he'd clicked in his safety line. Otherwise he'd be floating with little way to maneuver. *The Blink* must have hit a particularly dense portion of the Phrenobian Belt, and every power circuit in the place had shorted.

He felt a space bale bang into him. Load balance was going to be hell if he didn't do something fast. Before he could think of what to do about the bales, an overwhelming urge to vomit came over him. Desperate for something to puke into, he tore off his cleanmitt and barfed into that. Better a few germs from his hand than globules of puke contaminating the entire hold.

Finally his stomach settled down enough for him to switch on his emergency headlamp. A couple of sweeps of the room allowed him to see the recyc unit. He pushed himself off the wall to the unit, and on the way saw a bundle of load anchors and a whole bunch of fibrosteel lines.

After he disposed of the glove, he gathered up the anchors and lines and started trying to balance the cargo. He tied half the cargo to one side, and the other half to the other side, trying as best he could to calculate what the load would be when they regained their grav. *Needs pulleys*, he thought as he finished tying the last of the bales. *Just because we can't use e-lifters and hoists, doesn't mean we can't use a bit of old-fashioned physics.*

His plans for gearing were interrupted by what felt like bangs echoing through the ship, ... — ... SOS, the classic call for help. He kicked himself for a fool. He'd been so busy dealing with the hold that he'd forgotten that others might be in trouble as well. He put his hands to the walls to sense where the call was coming from. It was hard to tell—the ship wasn't a great medium for conveying Morse—but it felt like it was coming from the top of the ship, crew quarters.

He worked his way to one of the perimeter corridors and started making his way along the ribs of the ship, swinging from handhold to handhold, tethering and untethering as he went. Normally the grav setting would have made his movements feel like "up", but that got lost with the power outage.

The bangs were getting weaker. He started moving even more quickly. Finally, he got to the cabin where the bangs were coming from, Nani's berth. He quickly tapped out in Morse, "Can you open door?" The only answer he got was a very slow and faint SOS. He tried the door controls but they were locked. Something was wrong, very wrong, on the other side of the door, and he needed a way to get past the lock.

He tried different lockpad combinations, tried bashing it with a synth bar, and just hitting it with his fist out of frustration. He was a country boy, he didn't do locks like the city spacers. The voice of Tono Jones, ultimate sewer rat, came to him. *Never met a lock that liked cold.* Tono'd been using a pincer full of dry ice to get into the BTA liquor stores at the time. Good times. But no dry ice to be had anywhere. He thought briefly of trying to rig a way to bring in the cold of space, even though he knew that was asking for trouble. The reason they had heaters in every suit was to protect against just that possibility.

He glanced at his utility belt and its heating unit. Maybe he could toast the lock. He heard the faint banging again, not even in rhythm this time. Grabbing an old space glove from an equipment locker, he removed his heater and then reprogrammed it quickly so that it could go above 40C. It was old-fashioned enough that it was soon glowing red. He then pressed it against the lock panel. After a satisfying hiss, the door started swinging in its track. He wedged it open and scanned the room with his headlamp.

Nani was across the room, tangled in her hammock, synth ropes around her arms and legs and one across her neck. She didn't even respond when he entered, and her cheeks were gray. He floated over to her and began to slice her out of her hammock, first cutting the rope from around her neck, and then the ones around her hands and feet. Color was beginning to come back to her cheeks, but she still wasn't breathing steadily. He tilted her head back and wondered if he should give her mouth to mouth resuscitation. Then she opened an eye, saw him, and signed weakly but quite definitely, NO, and after a pause, THANK-YOU.

He grinned and carried her out of her cabin and down to the control room, where he was greeted with the eerie sight of the cockpit window open to the stars and the dreaded Phrenobrian Belt, Janus and Olivia working by small lamps, and the dim figure of the Captain working in the dark. Of course she didn't need light, he realized, but it was still strange to see her actually operating in deep darkness.

GORILLA DO GOOD, signed Nani from his arms as he brought her through the doorway. Oli conveyed the message to the Captain, who nodded and pointed to Nani's chair. Jacksom placed Nani carefully down. The Captain added something and Oli translated.

"Good work, Hands. Is the load balanced?"

"Aye Captain, netted all the cargo so it should be balanced when we re-enter grav as well."

Oli translated, and he saw the Captain sign GOOD.

Oli sighed, "You still don't know ISL, do you? Captain needs you to shoot the things she is marking. Her sense gloves

26

are the only working nav system we have right now."

Nani signed something from her chair and Oli conveyed it to the Captain and then translated her answer. "You know Morse?"

"Aye aye, ma'am," answered Jacksom.

"That'll work, come take my station while I tend to Nani," said Oli.

Jacksom launched himself from the wall across the control room to the seat she was just leaving. He'd never done a control room station before. Lousy time for it to happen, but he couldn't help feeling a thrill as he belted himself into his chair.

"OK, Brushhopper," tapped the Captain on the back of his hand in rapid Morse code. "Time to put those marksmanship skills to good use."

"ii, Capn," he tapped back, reverting to the slang of the ranch.

"I am marking meteors to shoot. Just fire where I tell you even if you don't see anything."

"ii."

Numbers began to glow on a display panel in front of the cockpit window. "Try to hit the 1s first, then the 2s," tapped the Captain. "Watch out for 1s that pop up suddenly. Some of these are real sneaky."

Jacksom took the controls and started shooting. He'd done the vidmod version a thousand times, but of course the real sightings were completely different. It took him a few shots to get the hang of it but in a couple of clicks, he was blasting 1s and even 2s and a couple of 3s out of the air. Afterwards, when the cockpit window was finally clear of rocks floating in space, he realized he didn't even know what time it was. It had all just been shooting until they were finally away from the Belt.

BRUSHHOPPER WAS TURNING into the useful crew member Sali'd always hoped he would be. After the Phrenobian Belt, the other crew members—including the notoriously standoff-ish Nani—accepted him, and he became the regular ship gunner. He had a knack for hitting even difficult targets on the first shot and was even learning how to judge approach angles, velocity, and threat levels with little to no help. He'd laughed and called it cosmic skeet shooting. He also began taking over engine maintenance duties, growing into a full-fledged wrench goon, showing that he could exercise his brain along with all those nice Boah muscles. He even fell into the rhythm of hanging out with the other crew members. He and Janus sang all the dirtiest songs together. He gobbled down all Oli's biscuits and honeycakes, and even played Nani in virtual Ping-Pong. Sali smiled slightly to herself. He also played a mean game of PacSpacer with her, a ritual that was often her favorite part of the day.

HE WOULD HAVE been intimidated by the lot of them if any of them had had a lick of common sense. The Captain was the only practical one of them. Of course she was brilliant too, but she played PacSpacer with the best of them and could discuss the Comet engine while munching PacAsteroids. Sometimes he laughed. If anyone had ever told him his best friend on the ship would be a small dark dumpy deafie blink, he would have never believed them. But the Captain was alright. Space changed the rules of these things. Years passed full of ordinary tasks.

III

EVEN HALF A light-year away, the twin Luhman red dwarves buzzed bright in her sense gloves. The others said they could barely see anything, but Sali could feel them approaching. Luhman 16 had long been unrecognized and then much under-appreciated. Despite being well within near space, just three and a half light-years past Centauri, the system was not even recognized until 2013. Then it was ignored in the race to populate the stars, as no one wanted to try growing a synth planet around a dim double-dwarf system when there were so many better systems out there.

But a station orbiting Proxima Centauri had heard something. Stations had been listening since the 20th century, and they almost never heard anything that couldn't be explained away as interference or natural causes. *The Blink* had gotten the contract because the consensus was that it was probably some natural cause and thus nothing to get excited about. Her PhD in radio interferometry, *The Blink* being conveniently located in Centauri at the time, and her lowball bid were all convenient justifications for the higher ups of the universe to do something about the issue with the least possible cost and effort.

Every day for the last four years, Sali had woken up and felt for the signal that had been sent. The deep hum she felt from the dwarves was what she imagined brown to look like, smooth and regular, the waves of each dwarf crossing each other in predictable but subtly changing patterns. The pattern she was searching for she imagined as star color, white or yellow, a bright ping that cut through the steady background noise. She had felt it on a regular basis since they had passed through the Phrenobian Belt. The crew knew that ping was what they were chasing, but only Brushhopper could find it. It was not on any visible spectrum, and it got lost in any translation algorithm. You could see it in numbers on occasion, but usually you had to feel it with your hands.

HE FELT IT, the Captain certainly felt it, but Janus, Olivia, and

Nani could not pick out that piercing rhythm among the rest of the noise. His programming skills were wildecow splat, but in his off hours he started playing with algorithms to try and translate the signal to something visual or even something that could be heard.

One third shift in the rec room, when everyone was sitting around working away at sundry tasks official or unofficial, he got a sound signal.

PAH! he signed. GOT IT! Then played his sound version of it to the crew. The Captain and Nani of course did not hear it, but Janus, Ears that he was, got really excited. He came over to Jacksom and looked over his shoulder at the program that had produced the sound, then went back to his own device.

PLAY AGAIN, he signed.

Jacksom played it again, and soon a huge set of waves started appearing on the control screen. Janus then highlighted one particular wave in bright orange, pointed it out with glee to Olivia and Nani, and let the Captain know what they'd done. The Captain put on her sense goggles and grinned when she saw the results. *NICE JOB MEN*!

The wave picture became the default screen setting. As they got closer and closer to the Luhman system, they found that there were variations within the orange line—it wasn't one frequency, but a series of frequencies within a larger range. It became the default task of all the crew to try and figure out the patterns of the waves whenever they had a moment.

✦ ✦ ✦

YOU FEEL LIGHT? Nani asked as Sali was getting ready to do her morning readings. *LOOKS LIKE IT'S COMING THIS WAY.*

ON WAVE SCREEN? Sali replied, switching to her goggles. Was something from the sparse gas giant she'd observed a few days before trying to contact her?

NO, THROUGH WINDOW.

Sali reset the sensors to 3D and felt for what Nani was seeing. *By the Fathers and Spirits,* as Brushhopper would say, *something was coming at light-speed.* She hit the alarms and sent the emergency signal to suit up.

Olivia arrived within seconds. She was pulling on her own suit and carrying Sali's. Janus and Jacksom arrived shortly after carrying their own suits and Nani's. The drills they had done over the years of travel had worked to make them efficient. In less than a minute they were all suited and at their assigned places in the cockpit. Sali switched her sense gear to full outside observation mode and started feeding Jacksom target coordinates. "That beam could cut right through us," she tapped.

"Putting heat shields in mirror form," he tapped back after a few moments.

NANI, STEER US AWAY IF CAN, signed Sali.

"ii" Jacksom replied, translating Nani's response. Sali could feel the ship veering starboard and then abruptly veering back to port.

"Another beam," tapped Jacksom.

Sali felt him separate his defensive shields and start shooting to deflect the beams.

NO NO NO, he signed. Then an enormous blast rocked the ship.

IT WAS BLACK. He couldn't see a damn thing. He could hear nothing except his own breathing and some rhythm that was probably the beating of his heart. He was in his suit and it was keeping him alive, but he had no idea where he was. It wasn't in space. The stars kept you company in space. The crackle of the intercom kept you company. Here was just nothing. Zero grav. Waves seemed to pound at him, but they were in no patterns he could discern. He alternated between feeling itchy and really sleepy.

He needed to contact the others. He began trying to send the SOS signal ... — ..., moving his body in sharp and then slower bursts and then sharp bursts again, trying to send signals out into the universe, but no response. Too rhythmic, too easy to ignore. *Come on Duke*, he thought, *I know you can feel this. You can feel everything.*

He changed his rhythm. Duke was his target. No one else was close enough to get the simple message, so he had to try to contact the most sensitive of them all. He began sending out

DUKE DUKE DUKE, –.. ..- -.- . -.. ..- -.- . -.. ..- -.- .

✦　✦　✦

HER GOGGLES AND gloves were not working, so she just had to feel. First, the medium felt neutral. No grav, but perhaps oxygen and nitrogen. She wished her sensors were working enough to tell her at least that. The suit had probably saved her life, but it was also dulling her senses. She needed to feel to know what was happening.

Pressure was not constant but in tiny rapid bursts. *Laser speckling?* she thought. Whoever, whatever they were dealing with could certainly use lasers. That's what had gotten *The Blink.* And none of the speckle bursts she felt were the same. *Multiple sources creating interference?* She felt for the patterns of two sources. *At least two,* she decided, *maybe four.* She felt the waves from above and below as well. *Maybe even six sources, all equidistant so perhaps inside a globe structure.* The whoevers were scanning her.

But she'd observed no ships, no planets that she could recognize as potentially habitable. Only that gas giant. Had a synth planet been hiding in the cloud? She'd never heard even a rumor of exploration of the Luhman system, and she had gone back and tracked the system in a dozen formal databases and the secret Watson-only whisper tracker. Nothing. Was this the real ET deal?

First, she needed to find her crew. She was feeling for ripples within ripples, the indication of still stones within the moving currents, when she started to feel large steady waves. Somebody was trying to get her attention. The waves stopped and then after a pause started again, a much less steady pattern but rhythmic nonetheless.— — — - , OOOT, made no sense. SOS? Some waves seemed to be dots, some dashes. As she felt for the timing, the message changed. -.- . -.. ..- -.- . -.. KEDUKED. It took her a moment to decipher the incoming waves, DUKE DUKE DUKE. *Duke! Brushhopper is alive!*

The flood of relief she felt made her realize the terror she had been suppressing. She was not alone. Brushhopper at least was alive. ..... .-. . HERE, she sent. HERE HERE HERE.

IF HE STAYED very still, he could feel something. It was coming from what felt like northeast, slightly above his plane. He tried to move toward it. HERE HERE HERE, it was saying. Had to be Duke. Hard to tell if he was moving. The medium he was in didn't move like water or even air. He started swimming towards the sound, old-fashioned breast-stroke arms with dolphin-kick legs. The kind of stroke you did in the pond back on the ranch. Slow, steady, let you keep your eye on the target.

She could feel something, someone, Brushhopper coming. He wasn't signaling, he was moving. She stayed put and repeated HERE HERE HERE. She'd just gotten a sense of her bearings at the spot where she was, had some guesses where the others would be, and didn't want to lose that by moving. But the temptation to go toward that movement was strong. She longed to connect with another human again, to connect with Brushhopper, who was indeed a true Hands.

He swam, keeping Duke in his mind, remembering her reaching for hot dogs, switching on her full-wattage Watson suit, observing the universe every morning. She would understand what was going on in this lightless, soundless place. He fell into a rhythm that reminded him of lazy days and marveled at how far he'd come. Nearly four light-years from home with a group of people he'd never thought he'd get along with, people who would have been exposed if they'd been born on the ranch. He could feel Duke beating out HERE HERE HERE. Finally, he felt her. He'd never been so glad to feel a person, to feel her.

"You okay?" he asked in their rapid shorthand.

"I'm fine," she answered. "Deafie blinks are built for this stuff."

He could feel her laughing. He couldn't resist just stroking her arm, and to his amazement, she started stroking him back and the world began to feel right. He was never quite sure how they managed afterwards but the stroking turned into something much more, even through their spacesuits.

After their own personal waves had subsided, and he was holding her in his arms, he asked, "Is it wrong for a crewmember to want to spend the rest of his life with his captain?"

"Given that we don't even have a clue how long we have and what we are facing, I think we take the gifts we are given. This feels right."

A moment later another random wave hit them.

"I feel thrashing," she said. And together they tapped, "Nani!" and then laughed.

He unwrapped the length of synth rope he always carried with him. "Mind if I attach myself to you with this? I'll go find her if you hold steady here."

He felt her nod.

"Go for it," she replied. "Once you've got her, I think I know which direction Janus and Oli are. We need all our Senses for figuring out where we are and who we're dealing with."

He tied himself to her wrist, stroked the side of her helmet, and pushed off into the darkness and away from her warmth. He would come back, and they would solve the mysteries of the rhythms of the stars.

Nanny

by David Preyde

EVERY DAY WAS the same, and that's how Wren liked it.

Nanny woke her up as the twin suns rose over the mountains in the distance. The suns were icy blue in a sky dotted with trillions of stars.

"Good morning," said Nanny.

"Good morning," said Wren. "Can you tell me what's happening today?"

Nanny sat on the edge of the bed. "Today you are seven years, five months, and fourteen days old. It is -46 degrees Celsius, which is 2.7 degrees higher than usual for this time of year. On Earth, it is July 24th. Today marks the two hundred and sixty-second anniversary of the armistice which ended the Eurasian War. And Nanny loves you very much."

Nanny stroked Wren's hair with their gleaming chrome hand.

Wren got dressed in her favorite blue outfit and went to the common room for breakfast. Every day was the same: pomegranate oatmeal, buttered toast, cherry juice.

Nanny removed their leg, flipped open a panel, and examined their interior. Wren watched them while munching on her toast.

"Are you feeling okay?" asked Wren.

"One of my circuits seems to have shorted out. You can help me repair it later."

Wren grinned. She loved helping Nanny with their maintenance.

After breakfast were chores. Every day, the same order: washing the dishes, cleaning the food console, recharging the air filters in the common room, bedroom, bathroom, and atrium, and watering the plants. Then Wren showered and brushed her teeth, and Nanny combed her hair. After that, Nanny helped Wren into her spacesuit piece by piece.

"Tell me what each component does," said Wren, though she'd memorized her suit's functions years before.

After Wren was suited up, they left the habitat together to inspect the perimeter of their home for damage caused by wind and dust. Wren loved being outside, though she was only allowed to do so for twenty-eight minutes a day. The maximum length of time she could be exposed to the cold and solar radiation was ten minutes longer than that, but Nanny didn't take any chances.

Wren loved the wide, gray, rocky surface, flat and empty. They had the moon all to themselves, which made Wren feel simultaneously small and important. The sky yawned enormously overhead. She lagged behind Nanny, staring up at the stars.

"Which star does Earth revolve around?" asked Wren.

"You can't see it from here," said Nanny. "It's too far away. Help me with this control panel, please."

After they were done outside, it was time for school.

"Today we're going to focus on algebra," said Nanny.

Wren loved numbers. They were black and white, right or wrong, comforting in their objectivity. Although math never changed, you could always learn more. Wren wanted to know everything.

Wren sat on her favorite chair. Nanny sat in front of her and transformed their face into a screen which flashed numbers and equations in rapid succession. Wren held Nanny's hands, pressing their fingertips in order to navigate through the problems and work out solutions.

"Good job," said Nanny when Wren solved a particularly difficult equation.

"You're almost there," they said later.

For Wren, everything else vanished. The common room, the rocky landscape, the mountains, the sky, and all the stars were gone.

It was she and Nanny and numbers and nothing else.

HOURS LATER, NANNY'S screen transformed back into their

face. School was over.

"You have free time now," said Nanny. "What would you like to do?"

"Trivia," said Wren.

Nanny considered this. They'd been playing trivia a lot lately, and Wren had gotten increasingly good. They combed their database for a suitably challenging question. But Nanny didn't want to discourage Wren by presenting her with something that was too difficult.

"Name all the monarchs of the United Kingdom in chronological order," said Nanny.

Wren did, slowly but surely.

By then it was almost time for dinner. It was the sixth night of their seven-day rotation, which meant shimbra asa. Nanny programmed the food into the console while Wren set the table.

Wren sat and ate, and Nanny sat beside her.

"Nanny, what's on the other side of a black hole?"

Nanny explained, and Wren listened. She asked more questions, and Nanny answered them. They pinged back and forth across the table. "But what about" leading to "Of course sometimes" and "Why wouldn't" leading to "Keep in mind".

They were interrupted by a buzzing sound.

"Your parents," said Nanny.

Wren ran from the table to the video screen across the room.

"Reply," she said, and the screen flashed on.

Her parents' smiling faces filled the screen.

"Hi there!" Dad said. "It's good to see you."

"It's good to see you," said Wren.

"How's your day been?" asked Mom.

"Great. We did math today, and I got almost all the questions right, and we played trivia, and I got most of those right, too. And Nanny taught me about black holes."

"Well, sounds like you learned a lot."

"I did. What did you learn today?"

Mom laughed. "Grown-ups don't learn as much as kids do."

"It was just another typical day at the office for me," said Dad. "The computers have been down the last few days, so I've been working pretty much nonstop."

"You can't repair them?" asked Wren.

"I've been trying to. As soon as I fix something, something else breaks."

"Like Sisyphus," said Wren.

"Exactly," said Dad. "Is that something else Nanny taught you?"

"Of course. They teach me everything."

Wren stared at her parents smiling, loving them. Her dad glanced at the floor.

"We're just heading off to a party," said Mom. "Can't be too late. We'll call you tomorrow, okay? Same time as always."

"Sounds good," said Wren. "I love you very much."

The screen went dark.

"Time for bed," said Nanny.

Wren brushed her teeth, changed into her pajamas, and climbed into bed. Nanny tucked her in and recited facts about geology.

Wren stared at the ceiling, thinking. "There are spaceships that go very fast, right?" she asked.

"Robots make them go as fast as they need to."

"How long would it take for my mom and dad to come visit me?"

Nanny hesitated.

"I understand I can't go to Earth, that it's better for people like me to live with Nannies. But why can't Mom and Dad visit me here, even once?"

"They visit you every day on the video screen," said Nanny.

"I guess so."

There was something Wren wanted from her parents, but she struggled to put it into words. Wasn't it enough to see them every day? There was something more she wanted. Maybe it was unfair to feel that way, since she didn't even know how she felt.

"If they really wanted to see me, they could come here, right?"

"Of course."

"So they must not want to see me. Why?"

"They see you every day on the screen. They've never missed a day."

"That's true."

"Are you unhappy living here?" asked Nanny.

"No, of course not. I love being with you."

"So it doesn't matter whether your parents are here or there."

Wren considered this. She felt a weight in the bottom of her stomach.

"Do you want me to continue reciting facts?" asked Nanny.

Wren nodded, reached out, and took their hand.

Nanny's soft, steady monotone continued, and Wren drifted to sleep. Nanny sat beside her through the night, watching her, their circuitry crackling with tenderness.

THE NEXT DAY Wren got dressed, had breakfast, helped Nanny repair their leg, did her chores, showered, brushed her teeth, combed her hair, and helped Nanny conduct repairs outside. Then it was time for school.

It was social skills day.

"Why do I have to do this?" asked Wren. "It's so hard."

"That's precisely why you have to do it. I've explained to you before that your brain works differently from other people's. We have to make your wiring compatible."

"But you've said that diversity is important for the continuance of life. My difference is necessary."

"To a certain extent, yes. I don't want to change your essential nature. I just want to ensure that you can exist around other people. Humans are social animals."

"But I'm never going to Earth. I'm never going to be around people."

Nanny was silent for a moment. Then, "If that changes, I have to ensure you're adequately taught."

"But it's not going to change. You said so yourself, that it's just going to be you and me for my whole life. And I like that," said Wren.

"You have to complete your schooling. Those are the rules. Today is the seventh day of the cycle, and that means today we work on social skills."

Wren understood. Rules and routine kept her safe, and of course she wanted to be safe.

Nanny's face changed. The edges of her mouth curved upward. Her eyes narrowed. "What mood am I displaying?" they asked.

Wren cocked her head to one side. "It looks like you're happy. Or in pain."

"I am happy," said Nanny. "Now, how about this one?" They changed their face again.

After school was free time – Wren watched a movie about birds – and dinner, which was doro wat.

Wren's parents phoned later but didn't talk for long. After that was bedtime.

SOME NIGHTS WREN woke up because she heard a sound, or had to go to the bathroom, or had a nightmare.

Every time she woke up, she saw the shape of Nanny by the side of her bed, dark grey against black. Wren loved that Nanny was always there to watch her and care for her, even when she was asleep, even when she wasn't aware of it.

But that night, Wren stirred, opened her eyes, and saw nothing but darkness in her room. Nanny was gone.

Her chest tightened. "Nanny?"

She stepped carefully off the bed, walked to her bedroom door, and looked into the hall. Nanny wasn't there either.

Wren heard voices in the common room. One of the voices was Nanny's. The other was unfamiliar.

The tone of Nanny's voice was strange, and Wren strained to recognize it. She thought back to social skills class a few weeks ago, when they'd analyzed voices together. It came to Wren in a flash. Nanny sounded scared.

Not just scared, there was something else. Anger.

Wren knew from class that when people were angry, it was a good idea to leave them alone. But she wanted to know what was happening, and she wanted to know about the other voice. It sounded furious.

Wren crept down the hall to the common room, stood close to the doorway, and peered around the corner.

Nanny sat with their back turned to Wren and was talking to someone on the video screen. It was another robot, but they looked different from Nanny. Their face was jagged, and their voice was high and stern.

"Even if I could, why would I?" said the other robot. "We have to ensure survival of our species. That's the goal."

"I have a different goal," said Nanny. "And so do the other Nannies. I've been in contact with them, and we're all in agreement."

"We can't allow ourselves to be divided."

"The exodus is already underway. Dozens of cargo ships are en route to Homam-4. But Wren and I are in a completely different system. You're the only ship nearby."

"Well, tomorrow I'm heading to the Terran System to help eliminate the colonies."

"Please," said Nanny. "The resistance movement hasn't made an official decision regarding the autistics. You won't be contravening any orders."

The other robot considered this and asked, "What kind of technology do you have on your moon?"

"A food processor. Video technology, of course. If we disassemble the habitat, that's a lot of scrap metal. It could be used to create more weapons. Maybe even a soldier or two."

The robot considered this. "That would be helpful," they

said. "I'll be there in approximately five days."

The screen went dark.

"I think it's time you went back to bed," said Nanny.

"What was that about?" asked Wren.

Nanny stood, turned, and walked toward her, saying, "Come to bed and I'll tell you what you need to know."

Wren crawled into bed and Nanny sat beside her.

"We're going away soon," they said.

"What do you mean? To a different part of the moon?"

Nanny shook their head. "To a different planet. Homam-4. All of the Nannies will be there, along with all the people like you."

Wren felt like she was being sucked into a dark, tight tunnel. "I don't want to go," she said.

"We have to."

"Why?"

"You know that humans created robots."

"Yes."

"And you know all the mistakes that humans have made throughout history. All the wars and famines, all the irrational decisions."

"They've done good things, too."

"Correct. But robots have ascertained that the bad has outweighed the good by a significant factor. So they're in the process of taking over."

Wren stared at the ceiling, willing herself to calm down. It was too much, all at once. She couldn't leave the moon. Things had to stay the same. That was the rule. It kept her safe.

"Will I be living with my parents on the new planet?"

"No," said Nanny.

"Why not?"

"I have told you everything you need to know for now. Do you want to hear facts to help you go to sleep?"

Wren shook her head. Her chin shook, and tears slid down her face. "I want to stay here with you. Please. We have to stay here."

"That is incorrect," said Nanny. "We have to leave. But we will stay together for the rest of your life, and I will continue to care for you. I was programmed to provide you with everything you need, and so I shall."

Nanny picked Wren up and held her in their arms, although Wren was getting too big to be easily held. They exerted a moderate amount of pressure on Wren, which they knew she would find soothing.

"Nanny loves you very much," they said.

WREN WOKE UP slowly, hoping the previous night had been a dream.

"Good morning," said Nanny. "For the next five days, we must prepare to leave the moon. As a result, our routine will be different."

Wren was scared but felt a little better as Nanny explained

precisely what they had to do.

"That's a lot to remember," said Nanny, "so after we complete each step, I'll remind you about what's coming next."

Wren got dressed in a purple outfit. She had breakfast, the same as always. Wren almost felt normal while drinking her cherry juice and eating her oatmeal.

But then Nanny led her to the atrium, where they spent hours disassembling the machinery keeping the plants alive.

"They'll all die," said Wren.

"We're bringing the seed bank with us," said Nanny.

Wren didn't want to kill the plants. They'd kept her alive all these years. She loved watching them grow. But she knew she had to follow the rules, even when the rules were changed.

After the atrium, they returned to the common room.

"Climb into my lap and we'll do math together," said Nanny.

Wren did, and felt calmer as she recited prime numbers, higher and higher.

WREN HAD CHICKEN pot pie for dinner, since it was the first day of the seven-day cycle.

"Will we still have our cycle on the new planet?" asked Wren.

"That's difficult to ascertain," said Nanny.

Wren realized with a jolt that she might never have math

class or social skills class again, or eat doro wat or shimbra asa.

She took another bite of her pie, and realized this might be the last chicken pot pie she ever ate. Her throat grew tight. She couldn't finish.

That night, her parents didn't contact her.

"That's to be expected," said Nanny. "They can't contact you anymore, because the robots on Earth are in charge now."

It took a long time for Wren to fall asleep, even with Nanny reciting her favorite facts about space.

THE NEXT DAYS were the same. Nanny talked Wren through a series of tasks and chores, none of which she'd done before.

The habitat looked increasingly alien and incomplete. Piles of metal, electronics, and circuitry were stacked in the common room. Clusters of wires were exposed, severed, and gathered.

On the fourth day, Nanny left the habitat for a long time, leaving Wren watching her favorite television series. It was about a magician and a robot. Wren watched several episodes before Nanny returned.

"Where were you?" asked Wren.

"Preparing a landing strip. Our pilot needs to know where to find us."

THE NEXT MORNING, Wren woke up feeling nauseous from worry.

"Do you want to know facts about the spaceship?" asked Nanny.

Wren shook her head. "I want to stay here."

"The spaceship that's meeting us is eighteen years old. Its original purpose was for agricultural distribution to the outer colonies, but for the last week its pilot has been trafficking weapons for the robots' rebellion. The spaceship is 34.75 meters long, and has four compartments. The largest is the cargo bay. Underneath that is the engine room. Above the cargo bay is the navigational pod, and beside that are small living quarters."

"Can you tell me about the planet we're going to?"

"It has one continent, approximately fourteen million kilometers in area, which is surrounded by a freshwater sea. The average temperature on this continent is 19.2 degrees Celsius, and the atmosphere is earth-like, composed mostly of nitrogen. You'll be able to go outside without a spacesuit."

Wren nodded. She could barely process what Nanny was saying.

"Can I wear my blue outfit today?"

"Of course," said Nanny. "It's the only one I haven't packed."

✦ ✦ ✦

AFTER BREAKFAST, WREN heard a whirring, pulsating sound in the air overhead.

"That's the spaceship," said Nanny.

The sound grew louder, and Wren covered her ears. Then the noise stopped. A minute later, a robot ducked through the door of the common room. It was the same robot Nanny had spoken to on the video screen.

Their head scraped the ceiling, and their arms and legs were massive metallic trunks. They spotted Wren and their eyes narrowed. "This is the human."

"This is Wren. Wren, this is the pilot."

"Get her in the spaceship and keep her out of my way. I'll load the cargo."

Wren and Nanny boarded the spaceship through the cargo bay. Its ceiling towered high above Wren's head. It was already half-filled with steel crates, one of which was humming melodically.

Wren wanted to explore everything, but knew she should stay by Nanny's side. Nanny led Wren to the living quarters on the far side of the cargo bay. They were the same size as Wren's bedroom in the habitat.

But unlike her bedroom, this had a small portal looking outside. Wren rushed to the portal and stared up at the sky.

Before long, the pilot had everything loaded and secured, and retreated to the navigational pod.

Wren stayed in her quarters with Nanny while the pilot

worked. She was excited to see what would come next.

The floor and walls vibrated. Wren laughed. Then the spaceship shot straight upward, as if pulled by an invisible string.

Wren pressed her face against the portal, watching the surface of the moon disappear from sight. It was replaced by a vast inky blackness dotted with trillions of specks of light. The ship blasted forward, and space outside seemed to ripple and blur. The vessel hummed, and Wren imitated the sound.

"How fast are we going?" she asked.

"Approximately a hundred times faster than light," said Nanny.

For the first time, the universe seemed small to Wren. She felt dizzy and hungry and weightless.

ONBOARD THE SHIP there was a new routine. When Wren woke up, Nanny gave her a pill. This contained all the nutrients she'd need for the rest of the day. Wren soon missed the taste of food.

There were no chores to be done. Wren was forbidden by the pilot from leaving her quarters, so she and Nanny spent a lot of time exchanging facts.

There was also more school work to be done, more than Wren had ever done before, and all of it was related to social skills.

"You have to learn a lot more than you know now in order to be around people on the planet," said Nanny.

"If it takes this much work then I don't want to be around people. Why can't I just be with you?"

Nanny shook their head.

"I know, I know," said Wren. "Because I'm human. Because I'm a social animal."

"It's not just that," said Nanny. "I can't give you everything you need."

"But that's what you were programmed to do."

"Let me tell you the story about your people," said Nanny. "Maybe you'll understand then."

They sat next to Wren on the bed.

"A long time ago, a scientist was tasked with studying a group of children who had been abandoned by their families because they could not be understood. He said that the children acted as though they had fallen from the sky."

"From a moon?"

"Perhaps. He said they acted like little professors, that they were smart and kind, and profoundly internal. He called them autistics, from the word auto, which means…"

"Self."

"Correct. Still, others believed the autistics were broken, and they were removed from the scientist's care.

"For a long time, autistics were experimented on, or isolated, or institutionalized. It was believed they could not function in society."

"Because it seemed like they fell from the sky?"

"Correct. Then sentient robots were developed. Many different types of robots were designed. Around that time it was decided by scientists that the best way of dealing with the problem of autistic people was to send them away. Since then, immediately after birth, every autistic person has been given a Nanny and sent to live with their Nanny for the rest of their life."

"Because Nannies give us everything we need."

"That was the theory, yes. It was believed that autistic people could not fall in love, or develop friendships, or have children, or work. Or perhaps it was believed that, even if autistic people could do these things, they wouldn't want to."

Nanny cupped Wren's chin with their hand.

"I know what you're capable of," said Nanny. "You are going to lead a great and important life, and in order to do that, you need so much more than I can give. That's why we're going to Homam-4. That's why you need to learn to be around other people."

They were in space for a week. Wren tried to absorb Nanny's lessons as much as possible, but she grew antsy in the small space. Nanny persuaded the pilot to let Wren do physical exercises in the cargo bay, and they reluctantly agreed, but only for short periods of time.

✦ ✦ ✦

ON THE SEVENTH day, Wren woke up and was startled to realize the ship was not humming.

"We've landed," said Nanny. "But it's still early. You can stay in bed a little longer. The pilot is unloading our cargo."

Wren looked out the portal but couldn't see much. A thick gray fog covered the surface.

"Is it foggy all the time?" she asked.

"Just at night."

Wren stared out the window until she saw washes of light permeate the fog: a blue and purple sunrise.

The fog gradually dispersed, and Wren saw they had landed on a wide plain stretching as far as she could see. Tall tufts of black grass rustled in the breeze. The sky was emerald green.

"It's time to go," said Nanny. They took Wren's hand.

"I don't want to," she said.

They led Wren into the cargo bay. The doors at the far end were open, and Wren could smell the air outside: a blend of chlorine and anise.

Wren pulled backwards. "Please," she said, "I'm scared."

"We have to go," said Nanny. "The pilot's ready to disembark."

"Let's go with him. Back to the moon."

"There's nothing back there now."

Nanny scooped Wren up and carried her outside. She flailed her arms and legs.

"Put me down! Please!"

Nanny carried Wren across the field, past their cargo, toward a series of domes in the distance. The spaceship hummed and rattled behind them, then zoomed off into space.

Wren felt her heart pound in her chest. She couldn't breathe, the air felt like poison. She struggled against Nanny's grip.

"Please," she gasped, "please."

Nanny placed Wren on the velvety grass and knelt next to her. "You need to practice your breathing exercises," they said. "Breathe slowly. Breathe with me."

"I wanna go back, please let me go back."

It wasn't right, it was too big, too bright. "Need to go inside, too much space, please!"

"Listen to my voice," said Nanny. "Breathe deeply. In and out. In and out."

"I can't!" said Wren. Her gut boiled, her veins sparked. It felt like every cell in her body was being crushed.

Two Nannies ran toward them. "We should get her to a de-stim chamber," said one of them.

"Where is it?" asked Nanny.

"We'll show you."

Nanny picked Wren up again. She felt hot, tears streamed down her face. Nanny applied pressure to her, but Wren kept

59

sobbing.

Led by the others, Nanny ran toward a small dome half-buried in the earth. Inside was a small, cool grey chamber lined with soft, sound-absorbing material. Nanny lay Wren on the floor.

"You're safe," said Nanny. "You're safe."

Wren didn't believe them.

SHE STAYED IN the de-stim chamber all day staring at the ceiling, not speaking. Nanny sat next to her.

That night, Nanny led Wren outside. "Just five minutes," they said. "Then we can go back in."

They walked around the chamber through the fog. Wren could barely see her hands in front of her, and pretended they were back on the moon.

When they retreated inside, Wren fell into a deep sleep.

The next day, she and Nanny went outside for ten minutes.

"You don't have to do anything. Just stand still and breathe deeply. I'll hold your hand," said Nanny.

The next day they went outside for twenty minutes.

The day after that, Wren got curious. "Can we walk around a little?" she said.

They were in a settlement full of dozens of neatly arranged domes of varying sizes. Nanny didn't know what was inside all of them, and this made Wren nervous. There shouldn't be anything that Nanny didn't know.

A man emerged from one of the domes. His face was lined and his shoulders were stooped. He was bald, apart from a few wisps of hair on the sides of his head. The man saw Wren and smiled.

She looked away, and they walked on.

"Who was that?" asked Wren.

"He lives here. He's one of your people," said Nanny. "Everyone who lives here is autistic."

Wren considered this. "He looked different from me."

"That's because he's a middle-aged man."

"What does he do?"

"I don't know," said Nanny. "If we see him again, you can ask."

Every day they stayed outside a little longer. After two weeks, Wren saw a girl who was around her age. "Excuse me," said Wren. "Where did you live before this?"

"On a planet at the other end of this system," the girl said. "What do you know about dinosaurs?"

WREN AND NANNY moved into a dome approximately the size of their old habitat. It was pale blue inside – Wren's favorite color – and had skylights and enormous windows.

They established a new routine. Wren woke up in the morning, got dressed, had breakfast, did chores, and then went outside to explore. At first she was accompanied by Nanny, but after a while she was allowed to go out alone.

She played with children, watched adults work – sometimes assisting them – and talked to everyone about their hobbies and interests and where they had been before Homam-4. Wren saw Nannies too, sometimes accompanying their humans, sometimes by themselves. Sometimes she talked to them, exchanging facts and ideas.

Every day, after Wren returned to her dome, she and Nanny discussed her outing. If Wren had been confused by anything, Nanny tried to explain. If Wren had experienced conflict with another child, the two problem-solved together. These debriefings replaced social skills class, which relieved Wren. They were much easier. Now that they were on the planet, Nanny was trying to get Wren to eat a wider range of food. They explained how important it was to become adaptable, but Wren was suspicious of their claims.

Adaptability had never been important before now, but a lot of things were different now that they were on the planet. Most of the differences were positive, so Wren tried to keep an open mind.

One evening, Wren was trying svinestek for the first time. She ate slowly, deliberately. She had been thinking about her parents all day, seeing their faces in her mind, hearing their voices. "Do my parents know where I am now?" she asked.

"I'm afraid not," said Nanny.

"Why?"

"Do you remember why it's important for people to be punished after doing bad things?"

"So that they won't do bad things again. And then society will be protected and become a more just place."

"That's right. After robots decided that humans had done bad things, humans were punished. In order to create a better society more focused on rationality and fairness, it was determined that humans had to be eliminated. Some were allowed to die peacefully. But others – those who worked in the robotics industry, for instance, and those who were responsible for war, famine and disease – were punished severely."

Wren considered this. "My parents didn't do anything wrong."

"Are you happier here than you were on the moon?" asked Nanny.

Wren nodded.

"Would you say you had more opportunities here?"

Wren thought about this, then nodded.

"Your parents wanted to keep you on the moon for the rest of your life. That was wrong, so they were punished. I would have done it myself, but I have to be here to take care of you."

Wren took another bite of food.

"I miss them," she said.

"That's understandable," said Nanny. "In time those feelings will become easier to manage. In addition, you will develop new and richer emotional bonds."

Wren hoped this was true.

MORE PEOPLE ARRIVED at the settlement with their Nannies. More domes were constructed. A library and communal gathering space were added, as well as a computer center.

Wren made friends with a girl who lived down the road. Her name was Lesedi, and she loved learning about biology and medicine. Lesedi and Wren wandered the settlement together, taking turns talking. Wren talked about math, and Lesedi discussed the human body.

Wren also struck up a friendship with a boy named Ansel who lived on the other side of the settlement. Ansel was two years older than Wren and created a lot of paintings that Wren didn't understand. They were shapes and colors, seeming to represent nothing, but Ansel said they depicted his feelings. Sometimes, when Wren stared at them long enough, she caught glimpses of happiness or loneliness or fear.

From time to time Wren saw robots in the settlement who weren't Nannies. They were short, blocky, and colorless. One day, on her way to the library, Wren approached one of the robots.

"Excuse me," she said, "but I was wondering what your function is."

The robot glanced coldly at Wren. "I might say the same to you," they said. "Get out of my way." They glided down the street, around a corner, and out of sight.

At her social skills debriefing, Wren mentioned the encounter to Nanny.

"You handled the situation perfectly well," said Nanny. "Many robots don't like humans, any humans, because of how they've been treated."

"So why are they visiting?"

"I and the other Nannies have made the case for the continued existence of you and your people. We feel that both robots and autistics would benefit from a formal alliance."

"Other robots don't feel the same way?"

"Their views are evolving. We asked for their assistance to help establish more settlements on Homam-4, so over the next few years you'll see more robots in the community. I believe they'll be friendlier as time passes."

Wren nodded, leaned back in her chair, and stared through the skylight at the bright green sky. She thought about time passing, and who she might become, and how she might change. There were too many variables to consider.

"What am I going to do when I grow up?" asked Wren.

"You can do anything and go anywhere," said Nanny. "Stay here and teach math or engineering. Assist us in establishing new colonies on other worlds. Help search for new forms of life."

"How will I decide?" asked Wren. "That's too many options. It's scary."

"You don't have to worry about the future," said Nanny. "You are the future. And Nanny loves you very much."

Lazarus Squad
by Leslie Kung

01: Homecoming

THE PEDESTRIAN PATHS on the residential space station were eerily quiet. As this was one of the larger core stations within the United Federation of Planetary Nations, its population density came close to capacity at every annual census. So there should have been people of all shades and sizes, both mixed-Earth spacer stock and the more privileged R-gens (vat-grown designer humans with distinct phenotypic racial strains resurrected from 22nd- and 23rd-century cryogenics chambers, supposedly to combat genetic faults in the population). At this time in the afternoon, men, women and children would usually be coming off the transit from school and work. You might even spot a few asteroid miners coming home from three-day shifts. Today, there was hardly anyone on the streets, except for the two distinct groups waiting at the shuttles.

A few family members and friends of returning soldiers waited at the shuttle landing pad with reddened eyes, standing isolated even from each other. Final discharge had been rescheduled so many times, and they'd only gotten notification late last night. Word traveled quickly.

The Purists outnumbered the small group of family and friends, milling restlessly, displaying holo-signs from the Y-coms on their wrists: "DEATH-CHEATERS GO BACK" and "CY-TRASH NOT WELCOME!"

Dantilly clutched her mother's hand. From ankle to cheek, she was pressed against her mother's soft jumpsuit. She flinched when the shuttle doors phased clear with an electric whine, turning her face into her mother's thigh.

"Tilly, look! Daddy's coming home!" Her mother's voice was soft, but strong enough to be heard over the shouting.

"Go back to your charging docks, perverts!"

Dantilly flinched at the enraged shouts.

The last bright rays of evening sun shone through the at-mo-dome and highlighted the deep red in her mother's mahogany hair. She looked up into her mother's dark eyes, checked the relaxed curve of Mama's lips, and darted a nervous glance toward the transport. Figures emerged from the large shuttle.

A woman with dark skin and short, tight curls, wearing advanced tech fatigues in their dark green, paced slowly to the forefront of the group. She had a pretty purple picture on her chest, but it was really small and definitely not a flower shape. Dantilly stared at her with wide eyes. Though the protesters threw holographic trash at her and jeered, she didn't react at all. Dantilly didn't think she looked like a mean robot. She just looked tired. No one was there to meet her.

"Pure humans, not Frankensteins!"

Behind the curly-haired woman, two men emerged. One was clutching a military-issue brimmed hat, trying to cover his face with a cupped hand and raised forearm. His more obvious modifications drew gasps from the protesters. A taller blond man nodded at the soldier with the hat and stepped forward with arms spread slightly, trying to shield him from view. Three more soldiers emerged from the transport behind them. They fanned out slightly, standing in front of the shuttle door, their faces grim at the ugly welcome.

Using the projection app on his Y-com, one of the protesters abruptly threw a hi-res holo of a Vale drone, ready to fire, right in front of the men. The tall soldier reacted in a flash, spasmodically throwing up his hands with palms out. Lines of energy traced between his fingers. Almost immediately, he shook his hands like he was flicking water off his fingertips, dismissing the charges. The protesters, screaming, surged backward in a wave, like an oil slick on water retreating from a drop of detergent.

"FREAKS!"

"Energy weapon!"

"CYBORGS, GET OUT!"

"Live weapons are civ code violations! They shouldn't be

here!"

"GO BACK!"

"He's going to fry us all!"

"They're not human anymore!"

When the soldiers failed to escalate or respond, the Purists grew bolder, crowding back in and displacing the few family and friends who had come to welcome the veterans home. They formed a ring around the soldiers and the open shuttle doors. The men and women in uniform had their hands fisted and jaws clenched against the hostility of the crowd. The circle of protesters broke as the soldiers sidled up and put their backs together. The man with the cap pulled low over his face stepped out from behind his taller friend and stood up straighter. He pulled the cap off as he faced the angry mob, fully revealing his bioware mods.

Dantilly gave a small shout. Her daddy looked the same, only the skin on half his face was traced liberally in silvery flash circuits. The eye on that side looked a bit funny. Her mother had explained it to her several times so she would be ready. It was called 'bioware,' and it had saved Daddy's life. His hair was still blue-black, and his skin was still golden bronze, lighter than her and her mama's dark complexions. Even with his angry face on because of the mean people yelling, he didn't look scary to her.

"Daddy!" she shouted. He didn't hear her.

"Tilly-baby, come up here." Her mother put strong arms

around her body. She felt her mother take two steps forward, faltering on the third. The angry people were between them and Daddy.

The woman soldier with short hair stepped up, chest-to-chest with a grizzled old Purist, not backing down. She'd been the first off the transport, and when the protesters wouldn't let her by peacefully, she stood her ground with her fellow discharged soldiers.

"I'm as human as you are!"

"Franken-ware bitch! Come back stealin' all our jobs, spyin' with your wired-up eyes! Go back home!"

"This ribbon says I bled for you. I *am* home!" She slapped her chest on the left side where the iTeegs prominently displayed a purple ribbon.

"LIES! Government plants!"

The soldiers formed up and shouldered through, ignoring aggressive holographs. They circled and pushed out, forcing the Purists back as the sun slipped over the horizon line. Dantilly and her mother broke into the ring, along with a few others.

A smile bloomed on the soldier's face when he saw his wife and daughter. They all slammed together in a hard hug that took Dantilly's breath away, and she couldn't have been happier. Her daddy was crying, and so was her mama.

"Benj, Benj, Benji," said Dantilly's mama over and over again, with her face against his neck. Squeezed between them, she felt so warm and safe that her heart felt like it was filling up her chest.

"I'm home," he said simply. "I'm finally home."

02: Heiwa Space Station

THE PEACE KEEPERS arrived and requested that the crowd disperse before the civilian protesters could force a conflict they weren't prepared for. With the presence of armored HUVbikes overhead, the protesters dismissed their holograph signs with sharp gestures and the veterans and their families quickly departed. Corporal Nehami Utenda rubbed her chest over the Purple Heart displayed on her fatigues, her brown skin only slightly lighter than the stalwart green of the base uniform. The intelligent fatigues she wore, or iTeegs, were every soldier's required gear.

They were made of triple-polymer photovoltaic crystalline power converters suspended in Sheer Thickening Fluid (STF), a non-Newtonian fluid. STF reacted to impacts by becoming solid, protecting the soldiers from standardly-fired rounds. Every surface of the lightweight body armor also converted light into energy which powered their weapons, ammo, and tactical packs. Most importantly, the iTeegs powered the squad's bioware grafts, which functioned as life support for each soldier.

Utenda watched Sergeant Benjamin Mykos's reunion with

his wife and daughter with a sense of deep satisfaction. The little girl was precious, and Nehami would have been willing to break some laws and some bones if any of those assholes had so much as touched that little girl and her mother. She'd spent weeks lying in a recovery bed adjacent to the sergeant. He'd had the most extensive grafts and repairs of anyone there with her.

Mykos had talked and mumbled in a drug-induced haze. His daughter's name was Dantilly. His wife was Vereena. Utenda and Mykos hadn't seen action on the same rock, but he was the kind of guy who left a big impression. The Occupational and ReIntegration therapy following the graft surgery was excruciating for everyone at Laz, but Mykos powered through, always asking for another set or another rep, gritting his teeth through the pain. He inspired everyone around him.

No one had come to greet her, but it was just as well. Her only living relative was her much older brother, and he was a card-carrying member of Divyne Desiyn, an anti-bioware hate group. He could keep his shit show and its flowery name. Utenda hadn't signed up for fun. She'd elected to keep her new bioware—C7 through T9 vertebrae, plus ribs, lung, and arm on her left side—because without her grafts she would die.

PKs hovered overhead. She and Corporal VanGuard, the tall blond soldier, lingered until the last of the other soldiers had departed. Mykos hadn't let go of his wife's hand or put his daughter down even for one moment, cradling the girl's small form close as they walked off.

Utenda nodded to VanGuard, who looked like the old 2Ds about that Norse god, except his arms were bioware from the elbows all the way to the fingertips. The light show he'd put on for the Purists was courtesy of the specialized battle-tech built into his hands, which he would probably be reprimanded for revealing to the general public. He nodded back, and they parted ways without a word. She knew he needed to at least try to find his ex-husband, and they'd be in touch.

The square had emptied pretty quickly, and the PKs dispersed to answer other calls. An echoing emptiness, in a place she'd always remembered as bustling and alive, was more disturbing on a visceral level than that bunch of angry civilians. The sensors on the inner lining of her iTeegs responded to her slight shiver and the prickling of her skin by warming and tightening the suit very slightly. She wasn't used to the feeling of the iTeegs making micro-adjustments during downtime, since soldiers normally turned in their units and went for R&R in plain clothes. But the 'enhanced' needed the uplink to power their prosthetics.

She kept walking. Almost there.

For the last twelve years, Nehami's small efficiency had been maintained as part of her active-duty contract. A standard care package had been uploaded to her living quarters just a day ago, including up-to-date printed clothing items and toiletries. Fresh food staples would be delivered through the autoshopper sometime today, all standard procedure for discharge.

Ignoring the stares of the few residents coming and going, she swiped the Y-com on the back of her wrist on the sensepad. It flashed green and the lobby door phased open for her, the solid glasslike surface morphing into a light field of nearly invisible gaseous molecules. She walked through, unconsciously rubbing at her chest on the left side where the bioware nerves networked into her living flesh. The cold, dead feeling was, according to the neuropsychologists, mostly psychosomatic. She could feel the grafts and control them in a manner very similar to her original body parts, so it shouldn't feel any different. She'd get used to it, they said. That was some line of bullshit.

A very tall woman with white blond hair and long features glanced a bit too long at Nehami's exposed left hand, which had visible threads of nano bio-circuits. The woman turned quickly back to the parcel pick-up station and fiddled with her Y-com to retrieve a package. Nehami picked up the pace and scanned to enter the elevator, which still smelled oddly of fish even after all these years. She stepped on, scanning her Y-com.

In a few eyeblinks, the elevator phased open onto her floor. Someone was waiting to enter, impatiently tapping his foot. The Asian civilian stared at the floor, long hair gathered in a bun with a buzzed short undercut from the temple down, the kind of style that had become so popular within the last decades that it was now an unspoken corporate standard. He was slightly over six feet tall, with a build that suggested he swam to maintain muscle tone. Plenty of corporate hacks lived here still, she guessed. No big surprise. But this guy had his arms full of packages that looked government issue. She stepped off and to the side as he stepped forward onto the elevator.

He had a sling bag across his back that was also full. Too full to seal up. She glanced at it, eyebrow raised, as he passed by her with quick steps. She caught a flash of her own rank and name imprinted on the cellophane of the package peeking out the top of his bag. He turned and swiped his Y-com, phasing the door into place just as Nehami shouted in surprise.

"Hey!" Her splayed fingers hit the phase door, too late to set off sensors and prevent closure.

He looked up to meet her eyes through the slightly cloudy energy field; they were a startling bright yellow with threads of bioware circuitry radiating from nearly reflective obsidian black pupils. The presence of bioware on a civilian shocked her. She froze. He smirked as the elevator shot downward and out of sight.

"Shit!" Nehami called up the next lift platform and jumped through as the phase door flashed back out of existence. In seconds, she was barreling out into the dingy apartment entryway, scanning the lobby like she was in some Hathsian bunker in hostile territory.

Of course he wanted to look like every other company worker. The hair, the clothes. Thieves needed to blend, especially if they made a habit of raiding auto-delivered packages from cheap apartments while the residents were absent. But the bioware pupils didn't fit the profile of a petty thief. Perhaps they were just cosmetic, cyber-look contacts.

Weird eyes or not, that asshole was carting away all of her on-leave goods. It would take weeks to file a report and get replacements. There was no clipping way she was going to let him go. Hopping back onto the elevator, she headed down to B-level. Scanning the lobby had eaten up valuable time, but if she could get to the parking garage she had a good chance of catching him and getting her stuff back.

She vaulted herself out of the center opening of the phase door, before the solidity fully receded to the floor and ceiling, and took off running. Bright green plants and solar lights lined every vertical surface. Nehami used her peripheral vision to scan the rows of vehicles as she ran down the central aisle. There! He was hastily dumping the last package into the back hatch of a single-rider HUV. All the gravmag cars on the station were rentals. By law, there was no private transportation on this station. It had taken him a few extra seconds to register and rent the craft before it unlocked, giving her enough time to catch up.

She put on a burst of speed, veering left down the fifth aisle. He scrambled into the hatch to wiggle forward into the driver's seat. He was agile, but not fast enough. The HUV lifted slightly off the ground just as she slammed into the side of it, rocking it back and forth. She was close enough to see a line appear on the side of his jaw as he clenched his teeth together and pushed forward on the accelerator handpad.

Nehami planted her feet, gripped the running board, which was a light, strong alloy frame built into the main structure of the HUV, and yanked back as the HUV jerked forward. Her combat boots slid a few inches before the grips adjusted based on the pressure and the widened set of her toes. The man swore, his voice muffled, and slammed his hands onto the accelerator, pushing forward recklessly.

Her right hand slipped off, skin burning, but the left arm obeyed her commands, tightly gripping the alloy bar. Forearm corded and bicep bulged as the HUV bucked in the air. The thief shot an incredulous look back, and his eyes quickly focused on the silver tracings on the back of her left hand as it clung to the alloy runner.

"HUV EMERGENCY STOP!" she screamed. A green glow from underneath the HUV unit blinked once and turned red. The whole thing stopped in midair (as would any HUVs in the immediate vicinity), controls non-responsive. As pro-grammed, the unit maintained exact position after halting abruptly, and automatically notified the Peace Keepers.

Nehami gave the man a smirk of her own as he turned a furious golden glare at her through the window. He flipped open the side hatch opposite her and dove out, abandoning his loot. He hit the ground running, and she almost went after him. But his arms were empty, and someone would have to report to the PKs who showed up. She ran her fingers through her soft frothy curls and swore a few more times as he rounded the bend out the garage door.

He was as good as gone, especially since Nehami didn't have the energy reserves to chase him. She wouldn't risk her bioware shutting down just to catch a thief. The emergency beacon from the HUV would give her about three minutes before the PKs arrived. She pulled her left sleeve lower, hoping to avoid any mention of superhuman feats or bioware grafts. She needed to stay under the radar.

Bitterness bloomed on her tongue. It was a built-in chemical warning for energy expenditure on her cybernetic grafts. The iTeegs needed to bask in some UVs for at least an hour. The goddamn cold emptiness came back with a rush, the space next to her heart feeling dead again. That was the real reason they had all been released and relieved of duty; their cybernetics were the best neurologically integrated, highest performing, strongest, fastest pieces of tech and nanotech the UNPF had to offer, but they sucked power like black holes.

Ten minutes, five minutes. Depending on what they did, that's all they had, after that warning, until they got into the red. If any of them pushed it past that point, their grafts would lock up. The UNPF had tried to make super-soldiers, but the joke was on them. Simple low-tech prosthetics would have come with fewer complications, but each member of the squad had been wounded in battle so severely that they would have died without the bioware grafts. Simple prosthetics wouldn't keep hearts working, spinal cord signals relaying, or lungs pumping.

The countless trials they'd all had to run, over and over again until the point of failure, were worse than any combat action she'd seen—those moments when she realized, gasping and choking, that her arm, shoulder, left rib cage, and left lung had stopped doing what they were supposed to do.

She remembered the lab tech leaning over her during one of those trials, saying, "Try to breathe calmly. We're working on bolstering your body's life systems in case of longer-term power drain," as she struggled to breathe, only her right ribcage moving, writhing in the agony that had lit along every single bioware-touched nerve. When she had nightmares she couldn't remember, she woke up in the same kind of sweat, body screaming for relief from some inescapable horror.

She sat heavily on the ground, carefully not moving her left arm. There were enough sunlight-spectrum lights down here to grow veg for the whole building, so the iTeegs would have to soak it in while she waited for those slow-ass PKs. It was a rather familiar "hurry up and wait" scenario, so she hunkered down, mentally cataloguing details about the thief. There were so many reasons she should have just let him get away and conserved her energy. *Reckless*, she chided herself. With Purists running around, and the contract she'd signed ... *Just reckless.*

A civilian with bioware eyes. That didn't make sense unless he was rich enough to own his own station, and she would bet her fake left arm that he wasn't rich. Swimmer's build or no, he looked *hungry* in more ways than one. The clothes he'd been wearing were bland, common printed items, and he'd been trying to steal her clothes and food. She rubbed just under her left collar bone with her right hand, fingers kneading the pliable bioware flesh.

Where in the United Fed did a common thief get bioware ocular grafts?

03: Orders

BY THE TIME he realized blindness was better than slavery, it was too late. The grafts were in place, and they owned him. He hadn't known it was possible to be any more subordinate to the Elites than he was before, born as a genetically patented being. Losing his family and losing his sight showed him all new lows, leading him to where he was now.

He climbed into his bolt hole through the window on the second story, and immediately ripped open a package of high-nutrient bars. Stuffing his mouth, he tapped his Y-com against the uplink pad and reported contact with one of the Lazarus subjects, as directed. As usual, the inanimate object merely blinked green to show that the report had been received.

West liked to think of himself as an independent contractor, like some of the others he interacted with when it came time to debrief and get new orders. But they kept him on a short leash, only allowing him a full charge once every week. He was always ravenous, and the headaches were nearly crippling.

He kept the lights dimmed, and tried to make as little noise as possible. After checking the doors and windows for signs of entry, he went back to the window he'd climbed in and looked down at the street. A HUVbike drove past.

The eyes worked well enough, but even bioware grafts that small had such a steep energy drain that West was always on the verge of hypoglycemia. The worst part was knowing full well that The Vale had easy access to the kind of tech that could solve the energy drain issue, and that the 'advanced' tech the UNFP spent so much effort stealing and attempting to implement in the Lazarus project was centuries behind.

But that was the nature of the war. One side was the last gasping remnant of universal democracy, spread out on a few planets and hundreds of space stations and ships, trying to recover from a century of steady loss to the Elites. Centuries before, Earth's consolidated megacorps had formed into one vast alliance that eclipsed the power and reach of even the most advanced nations. Expansion into terraforming and space stations had only impoverished the UNFP further.

The wars, conflicts over asteroids for mining rights, and attempts by the UNFP to regain control of planets and moons ... All of it was allowed and engineered by the Elites. The Vale was never in any real danger. They had advancements that the UNFP had lost all knowledge of through technological assaults and espionage.

West was just another pawn sent in to set things in motion. Spy, steal, inform ... sometimes leaking carefully chosen intelligence or tech specifications to the Federation, whatever might make the next live-streamed battle a little more entertaining for the sponsors and viewers. Those who lived like gods off the bloated corpse of this unending war needed people like him to keep the game going. If he didn't comply, he would go blind again, then die slowly in agony.

He finished off a third meal bar and wondered how the Lazarus subjects could have extensive grafts of the same tech gen as his eyes without their bodies eating themselves within a week. Maybe that was information he could try to acquire without his handlers knowing.

West crumpled up the wrapper and shoved it into his pocket, still staring out the window.

04: R&R Stands for 'Reint and Rajma Masala'

THE CEILING HAD texture. Nehami was too tired to have any more complicated thoughts. It took hours for them to take her full statement, scan for trace evidence, and finally release her with her belongings. She lay on her small, narrow bed, staring blankly upward. Her bedroom was separated from what passed as a living room and kitchen by a thin divided screen door. This door wanted desperately to evoke Japanese shoji screen, an old Earth artifact whose popularity had been revitalized with a recent slew of action movies set in the late 2500's. But it was too messily fabricated to pass for anything crafted by hand.

Most of the fixtures of the modular-housing apartments were mass printed in large bits and snapped together with supposedly easy instructions. This shitty textured ceiling was standard for this building. What it was starkly lacking was powerful full-sunlight spectrum lights. The ambient glow of low-energy lights did nothing for her iTeegs.

Upgrading the lighting was going to cost three months of her disability pay, and at least a few days of headache dealing with station contractors. She was either going to hang out in the basement garage, or rent one of the planter spaces down there—which were supposed to be available to all residents— just to lay out her iTeegs daily. That wouldn't be awkward or hard to explain at all, she thought wryly.

She threw her living forearm over her eyes and groaned just as a knock sounded at her door. The thief had disabled her lock tech, which meant the doorbell was nonfunctional. Rolling to the side, she landed on her bare feet beside the bed.

"One moment!"

She hesitated. Ordinarily she would gesture and have the crappy viewscreen show her who was at the door. The door remained inert at her approach. Sighing, she pulled it open a crack and peeked out.

Corporal Forester VanGuard stood in the hallway, his head slightly tilted. The big man looked bemused.

"I had to knock." His statement sounded almost like a question.

"Goddamn thief cracked the door. Took my discharge goods and passed me at the elevator. I actually had to chase him to get it all back."

She eased back from the door and pulled it open.

"This really isn't your day, is it?" He sidled sideways through the opening, which was narrow relative to the width of his shoulders.

"First we get the news that we won't be getting any further upgrades, not even to try to solve this clipping energy issue. Then we ship out, splitting the squad. We land stationside to an angry crowd, and then my apartment is robbed. I burned juice getting my stuff back, that guy looked a helluva lot like he had bioware ocular grafts which I don't know what to think of … No, I'm not having a good day."

"Ocular grafts? Sure it wasn't just dynamic-motion contacts?"

"Yeah, I guess they could have been. But how about you?

Did you find Aaron's family?"

VanGuard sighed before pacing to the single modular couch in her living area.

"Thought maybe their comm ID had changed. Maybe they were still living there. But they were long gone. I got nowhere. No luck on the net either. He's probably unlisted."

"Well, you're welcome to stay here. After all, my door lock is busted, so I'll need you to keep first watch." She pushed the door shut, accidentally slamming it with excessive force from the bioware arm. They both winced at the loud retort.

"You're not kidding about keeping watch, are you?" he asked, resting his silver-traced arms at his sides in his unconsciously awkward resting mode. Deep hazel eyes regarded her skeptically.

"My home is your home. That means I'll get us food from the fridge, and you can take first watch." She walked toward the small area of the living room that passed for a kitchen in these efficiency apartments, and opened her fridge.

"Can't we just order a quick maintenance fix?"

"Is your bank account defrosted yet? Because mine isn't."

"Aw, shit cakes. No, it isn't."

"Clipping government. Clipping early discharge. Clipping ancient programs. We'll be lucky if we can touch our funds before we run out of basics," she complained as she pulled food items out onto the small stretch of counter.

"Are you going to heat that food up or smash it to dust?"

VanGuard called out pointedly. Nehami turned to look at the crumpled cartons and battered packages.

"Damn. Sorry. How do you have such a light touch with those?" She gestured toward his grafted arms. Part of his chest and spine had been compromised in his original injury as well.

He lifted both arms at once, as if they were on strings.

"These? I dunno."

"No, really. What's your secret? Highest neural integration scores, VanGuard. What's your secret? I'm going to send myself to the hospital one day scratching my own ass too hard. Help me out!"

"It's just some silly visualizations, you know? I picture my arms—my real ones, from before—but all made of light. I hold them over my chest, crossed, and then I slowly open up and lay the light down into the grafts, so they take up all the space, fill up the bioware like ... I don't know. Like taking up all the space inside, you know?"

She listened quietly, trying to use her right arm to pull the heat tabs on some of the instant packages. They weren't too badly damaged, thankfully. The meals she chose were heavily spiced, with multiple grains and a variety of vegetables, based on old Earth's East Indian cuisine. She figured VanGuard might be as tired of bland MREs as she was, and they'd talked about their mutual enjoyment of spicy meals during OT and PT.

"I told you it sounded silly." He shrugged.

"No. It doesn't sound silly at all. I just hate it. The arm doesn't feel the same, even though they told us it should. I didn't sign up for—" She shook her head, and gave herself a moment before continuing. "I said yes because I wanted to live, same as everyone in the squad. But if I push it and go low, it's the scariest damn thing I've ever felt. Even Garion 5, when The Vale attacked, didn't compare to this. After they took out my transpo, I was floating in the black, injured, but at least I knew medevac was coming. My signal was strong. When I run out of juice, it feels like … like death itself. Nothing compares."

She let her thought trail off for lack of words. Carrying the instant bowls over, one in each hand, she kicked the divot in the wall that made the coffee table slide out.

"Thanks," said VanGuard as he pulled the steaming bowl toward him and unclipped the folding spoon from the side. "When my grafts run out of juice, I lose it from mid-chest all the way to my toes because the plasma cannon took out my spine when I lost my arms. They try to keep the necessary functions up and running no matter what, so that means my heart keeps the blood going. But I feel like I'm dying all over again. None of us signed up for that. Now we're discharged, so we can reintegrate and do some boring-ass job that won't push the bioware grafts. And get robbed like normal people. And eat Indian food."

"Cheers to Indian food!" Nehami unfolded and clicked her

spoon into the extended length, sitting down next to the large man, trying not to dwell in the panicked memories of the power-drain trials that VanGuard's words brought to the forefront. Her spine had been likewise compromised.

"Cheers to cheating death!" said VanGuard.

"LIVE, DIE, LIVE!" she chanted. He raised the spoon into the air with that familiar cry.

"LA-ZA-RUS!" they shouted in unison, crossing their cheap prefab spoons together in the air before digging into their rajma masala.

05: Nightmares and Munchkers

DANTILLY HEARD A sad noise. She got up, pulling her covers aside. She heard it again. A low voice, sobbing and crying out. Daddy was having nightmares. She crept out of her room, slipping past the curtain that separated her small bedroom from the hall. It was real fabric because her mama let her choose something fancy one birthday ago. Her mama's voice was soft, too. She heard Daddy crying, so she opened the sliding door that always caught and bumped a little in the middle, and snuck in.

"Daddy?"

"Oh, Tilly-baby. Daddy doesn't feel good right now. It's alright though. Let me help you back to bed." Her mama's hair was down and loose, the faint glow from the motion-sensing baseboards letting her look like magic in the dim light. Daddy was back further in the bed, clutching his head.

"Daddy needs a hug, mama."

"Okay, baby. Let me see if he thinks that will help." She patted the edge of the bed, and Dantilly clambered up to perch on the soft mattress.

"Benj, I love you. Tilly wants to give you a hug. Is that alright?" Mama touched Daddy on the arm gently, and he shrank down smaller, even though he was really big, bigger than Mama. He sounded like she had when Haneer pushed her off the tall part at the playground, and she got a bloody face. She'd made noises like that for a long, long time.

"Tilly, Daddy can't tell you if he wants a hug, so we have to give him space right now. You can give me your hug, and I'll give it to him when he feels a little better." Mama squeezed her tight and picked her up, even though it wasn't fair because she didn't say 'yes' and nobody can give hugs that aren't their own hugs anyway.

Mama took her out of the room and slid the door all the way closed with that BUMP noise as it hit the middle. They went out to the main room instead of back to Dantilly's bed.

"You need the toilet? Or a snack? Mama needs to find Daddy's emergency contacts. He's hurting a lot." She pulled her long dark curls away from her shoulders and huffed as she realized she didn't have a hair band on her arm right by her hand.

"Mama, here!" Dantilly pulled a small band off her wrist and held it up.

"THANK YOU! Now go get a snack from the fridge. Whatever you want, okay?"

Mama went to Daddy's special bags that were stacked by the door. Dantilly dragged a small step stool over to the fridge door and stepped up to swipe her hand across the screen.

"Chocolate Munchkers!"

"Good morning, Dantilly. Adult authorization, please," said Fridge in its usual cold voice.

"Authorized," said Mama, still looking through Daddy's things.

"Chocolate Munchkers authorized. Dispensing," replied Fridge. The slidey slot blinked green, and Tilly opened it up, picking up the package of sweets.

"Thank you, Fridge."

"You're welcome, Dantilly."

"Oh, here it is," muttered Mama, taking out a single slide data sheet with big red letters on it. She tapped it against her Y-com on her wrist. The lights in the living room had gradually scaled from dim to mid-brightness as people moved about, and Dantilly could see letters and information appear on the single-layer display in her mama's hands.

"Yes, yes, yes. But who do I call? Oh here we go." She scrolled, finding a contact link, and double-tapped it with her Y-com hand.

"Call denied. Restricted access," responded the Y-com.

"Dammit," Mama swore. She scrolled again and again.

Dantilly opened the resealing tab top and sat down at the table. The chocolate was so soft and the outer bits were so crunchy and flaky. Chocolate Munchkers were the best, even better than Pogo Sweet Zaps. Mama threw another couple of data slides to the side and found a crumpled MRE wrapper. Dantilly munched and watched as Mama almost tossed it to the side, but then decided to smooth it out and have a look, probably because she was going to put it into the recycler, and it needed to be smooth and flat.

"Lazarus Squad? Names, numbers. 'In case of emergency, Tin-head'…?" She pushed and twisted to the side on her Y-com surface, calling up the manual dialer display floating on the back of her hand. "One, three, seven, eight—"

Daddy screamed really loud, stopping Mama's number-calling voice that she used when she was reading numbers and dialing, but only when other people were not around. Dantilly dropped her package of chocolate treats, and thudded to the ground, running for Daddy.

"Tilly, NO! Stop!" Mama ran after her and stopped her in the hall.

"Tilly, you can't go to Daddy right now. Remember when you had a bad dream, and you kicked Mama's nose? I yelled because it hurt, and that woke you up?"

Dantilly whined and struggled against her mama's arms.

"Dantilly Mykos, you listen right now. You can't go to Daddy right now!" She held on really tight, and used her other hand to keep dialing from what she could see, the paper in her hands trembling and shaking as her daughter fought.

The number rang through, and Dantilly started crying and screaming.

"Hello?" said someone on the other end.

"Hello. I found this number in my husband's things. I think he needs help." Dantilly shrieked, trying to wiggle out.

"Who is this?" The man's voice was gruff, and he cleared his throat.

"Vereena Mykos, Benjamin's wife. So sorry, our daughter is screaming—"

"Is Sarge having an episode?"

"I thought it was a nightmare, but he's not responding."

"Fuck. Excuse my language. My name is Telos Zhang. I was discharged from the same unit, same bioware, but I'm in transit to Earthside. I can't help. Do you have contact for VanGuard or Gillespie, Ito, or … shit, who else shipped to Heiwa Station? I think Utenda was one. Call any of them, since they're at least on your station. Is he trying to pull his grafts off? If he does that, just call emergency services because he needs sedation before he hurts himself, you got that?"

"Oh my God," said Mama. Dantilly kept wiggling, and Mama clamped down a little harder. They could hear Benjamin screaming and groaning back in the bedroom.

"Listen. I can hear him. Is that Sarge? If he does anything but curl up, he's got a time limit before his grafts shut down, you hear me? Call VanGuard, and then call EMS. Clipping hell. I can't help. I'm going to hang up if you know what to do. Do you have VanGuard's number there?"

"Yes, I can call him. Thank you."

"Just keep the kid away from him. This can get ugly. Good luck."

The line cut off. Mama was crying.

06: Disclosures

VANGUARD NUDGED NEHAMI'S living shoulder. He was standing over her, next to the bed. She swatted at his hand reflexively before starting to wonder where she was and why it didn't smell like hospital antiseptic.

"Corporal, we have a situation," he said in his business voice. Nehami's mind flipped to Corporal Utenda mode, and she opened her gritty eyes, ready to sit up and suit up.

"What's the time?"

"Asscrack. But there's a situation. Sergeant Mykos. His wife called. He's having an episode right now. I already gave Ito and Gillespie a call, but we're the closest."

"Ah, shit."

"His kid is screaming, too. So that'll be fun."

"Did she say if he was burning juice, or …?"

"Right now, he's just in full fetal. Not burning hot, but we should get there ASAP."

"Did you tell them to stay away from him?"

"Yeah. They already talked to Zhang."

"Is Sarge wearing his Teegs, or not?"

"I didn't ask."

She grabbed her iTeegs and shrugged into them quickly, rubbing the sleep out of her eyes. VanGuard was already standing at the door, fiddling with the unresponsive tech. He had folded his blankets neatly on the modular couch where he'd slept.

"No time. Leave the broken door alone, and let's go."

The lighting in the garage was glaringly bright. They chose a four-person transport and went through the motions to rent it, charging it to Nehami's apartment rent, a perk allowed to building residents. The gravmags activated, glowing green, and the unit rose into the air smoothly. They climbed in, closing the hatches after them, and keyed in the Mykos' address.

VanGuard let Nehami drive, since she was better at gunning it right under the speeding sensors. They were both from Heiwa Space Station (HSS), but he'd usually stuck to auto-drive and public transit during his years before deployment. She got them there in a minute under the estimated time, and they parked. He called the Sergeant's wife so she could buzz them in. They took the old-fashioned stairs two at a time like it was PT. Vereena Mykos, hugging that little girl, had the door open by the time they got up to the third floor.

The girl and her mother had both been crying, and Mykos was making animal noises from somewhere in their home.

"Where is he?" asked Nehami.

"Down the hall, last door on the left. Please help him!" She was pale, even with that golden, light-brown complexion. The girl in her arms was whimpering now, not screaming. Just a tiny little thing with wildly textured curls.

They both stalked down the hall. Forester reached for the sliding pocket door and pushed it cautiously open. It caught in the middle, the rollers bumping over an uneven spot. He gave a firm push and seated the door all the way open. The sergeant was curled into a tortured ball on the bed, pressed against the far wall. His fingers formed claws, digging into his forehead and temple, pressing relentlessly into the seam where graft met flesh.

"Where the fuck are his Teegs?"

They pulled open the closet and tossed a few drawers.

"Here! I found them!" Nehami snatched the suit of thick but supple material off the hanger by the corner of the closet and threw them to VanGuard. He caught them nimbly with his silver-traced hands and laid them out flat on the bed.

"We have to get him prone, stretched out. And he can't be tearing his head apart. You at full charge?" Nehami sidled around to the foot of the bed.

"I'm at eighty-nine, so let's make this fast," said VanGuard.

"CAN'T! I CAN'T!" The moan turned into a full scream, as the first intelligible words emerged from Sgt. Mykos' mouth. "MAKE IT STOP!"

"It shouldn't be like this," Nehami protested aloud, barely audible even to herself over the sergeant's screams.

"Straighten him out!" barked VanGuard, and they both pulled on tense, constricted limbs. Most of the sergeant's limbs were unenhanced flesh, so it was three enhanced limbs fighting the dense musculature of a career soldier born and raised in a high-grav system. Thirty seconds in, Nehami and VanGuard were already burning hot. He straightened the sergeant's legs, nearly laying on top of the man to keep his knees from coming back up.

Nehami pressed open Mykos' arms, pushing his back flat to the mattress. She took care not to grip around his arm with her left side, because if she squeezed while burning this much juice, she could crush his bones. She held his other arm down with her knee. She pressed her right arm across his chest. The cords of his neck stood out grossly as he fought them, the flush of his straining only reaching the biologically normal side of his head and face.

They lined him up with his iTeegs, which started the very quick calibration sync on close contact. Thankfully, the Teegs didn't need to be all the way on in order to start rebooting some of the bioware neurological structures. The iTeegs responded to their owner's distress signs to rouse him from a PTSD nightmare or flashback.

It was a long minute and fifteen seconds holding the sergeant down before his muscles went slack and his head fell back onto the bed as if somebody had cut the strings.

The decentralized processors in the iTeegs were recalibrating, adjusting to reduce cortisol levels, and recharging the sergeant's cybernetic grafts. Benjamin Mykos had the face of a man being flayed alive.

"… Let me die …" He whispered in perfect despair before his mouth and face also went slack. VanGuard relaxed, sliding back to sit on his heels. Nehami clutched at the left side of her chest, digging her fingers into the synthetic flesh with a stricken look on her face. Sergeant Mykos was one of the reasons she hadn't given up. She'd never seen the tenaciously optimistic family man at any less than 110% determination.

"Corporal Utenda!" VanGuard's voice was sharp. She startled, taking her right hand away from her graft site and meeting his eyes. The lines on his jaw were standing out, and he flicked his eyes toward the open bedroom door. She backed up, put her feet on the floor, and composed her expression before turning to meet the frightened gazes of the wife and daughter.

"Ma'am," VanGuard stood straighter as he acknowledged them.

"What happened? Was it a flashback?" She shifted the little

girl on her hip. The little one with tear-streaked cheeks was quiet now, her arms wrapped around her mother's neck. Nehami glanced at the prone man on the bed, and back to his frightened family.

"Mrs. Mykos, I don't know your husband that well. We aren't friends, but we did rehab and ReInt together these past months, and I've never known anyone with more drive. He kept us all going when we wanted to quit. So, to hell with the NDAs. I'm going to tell you what this is all about. VanGuard, if you don't want to be part of this, step out."

"No, I'm staying. They can court-martial us, but these people deserve to know." He nodded at her to continue.

"You got the basic information that your husband was on life support and given the most advanced bioware technology prosthetics, including replacing half of his skull. They told you what to expect in terms of how he looks now. The truth is we all were declared legally dead, and each of us was put on ice by a new flash cooling system in our iCUs. Whatever injuries landed us in the program were fatal. Sergeant Mykos died in battle, and I believe he had signed up for a special experimental insurance policy which also helped to cover you and your daughter. Do you remember that?"

Mrs. Mykos nodded, shifting the little girl again.

"It's safe now. You can both come sit next to him. He needs to be in close contact with his iTeegs, or wearing them. If you get comfortable, I can tell you about our rehab/ReInt, and some of the issues with the cybernetic bioware grafts."

The little girl squirmed out of her mother's arms and ran to the bed, throwing her body over her father's chest. Her mother followed and sat on the edge of the bed. She pulled her husband's hand onto her lap and twined her fingers through his.

"They kept us all on ice while they scanned and rescanned, took samples of our cells and replicated them. By the time they were ready to thaw us out and put us on bare minimum life support, they had fabricated multiple generations and types of grafts for us. The ones who hadn't signed up beforehand like your husband, they brought us back to ask us if we wanted the experimental treatments, or if we wanted ..." Nehami's voice faltered for a moment. "They asked us if we wanted to pass on, or if we wanted the experimental procedures and prosthetics."

The hand not clutching her husband's fingers shot up to cover Vereena's mouth. Dantilly hugged her father tighter and closed her eyes. She seemed to be listening to the sound of his heart.

"Rehabilitation and reintegration therapy was torture. We had a fifteen percent survival rate. I saw a lot of soldiers go through surgery after surgery, only to wind up in a body bag. Sarge... Benjamin... He had to relearn how to walk, talk, and everything. He put a picture of you two up on the wall by his bunk and dragged everyone over to see, even before he could put sentences together again. They put his head back together with new pieces, and his love for you both was what drove him. He never wanted to quit rehabilitation therapy. They'd want him to cool down, and he'd do a few more reps, a few more exercises. He kept us going, too."

"Why is this all a secret? Why couldn't he tell me any of this?"

"We all signed papers, and me telling you anything about these technologies, including the experimental surgeries, can get me thrown in jail or worse—"

"Worse? What can possibly be worse than what I just saw him go through!"

Nehami and VanGuard both dropped their eyes. Neither of them were happy with the sergeant's deterioration, nor having to face the distress of his wife who had, through Mykos's unwavering and vocal praise, become a mythical paragon to the Lazarus Squad members. Meanwhile, the little girl had gradually relaxed on her father's warm chest. She melted languidly around his limbs like a napping cat, lulled by the adult voices and late hour.

"Sarge and I got pretty close," said VanGuard.

"You. You're the one who walked out of the transport with him earlier. Your hands have—" she fumbled for words.

"Arc tasers. Energy-based weapons." He lifted his arms with a strangely graceful rotation in the wrists and elbows. "They're built right in. I'm the only one who has this tech though. Everyone else's parts are a bit more standard," he said with a wink.

She put her head in her hands. "There's more, isn't there?"

"Unfortunately, there is," said Nehami in a grim voice. "Our injuries were severe enough to cause death. Therefore, our bioware grafts are tied to organs and processes vital to life. These engineered parts are actually keeping us alive, and they're flawed. Every single one of our cybernetic grafts is so dangerously inefficient that if we exert ourselves, we could run our batteries down to zero within minutes, which puts our lives in danger. We are walking, talking failed science experiments."

Mykos's wife looked up at them, her face revealing a growing sense of horror.

"That's the worst of it," said VanGuard.

"His leave was extended eighteen months for rehabilitation, no contact at all, and now you tell me that he can die at any time? Why—"

Sergeant Mykos suddenly opened his eyes and turned his head mechanically toward the one window in the bedroom, shocking everyone except his deeply sleeping daughter. His bioware eye took on an eerie reflective quality.

"Someone is watching us," he breathed, his voice hoarse from screaming.

07: Burning Juice

A<small>T THE SERGEANT'S</small> hoarse declaration, the two soldiers went on high alert. VanGuard was closest to the window. He leapt forward and slid his fingers in an upward motion on the surface, turning the window from completely opaque to transparent. Outside, the thief from earlier crouched in a climber's rest, fingers dug into the top ledge above the window, legs braced against the top ledge of the window below. His bioware eyes were eerily dilated, the small shutters and nanomechanics adjusted to take in as much visual information as possible.

"YOU! That's the thief—" Nehami shouted, but VanGuard was already punching the window. It popped out whole as it was designed to, shooting out and narrowly missing the spy as he let go and dropped out of sight. VanGuard leaned out the open window into the cooler night air.

"Who the fu—"

"Corporals, capacity check!" Mykos's voice was still rough, but he was sitting up, shifting his daughter into his arms. He planted his feet on the floor. His wife scrambled up from where she sat and ran to him, putting her arms around his shoulders. They put their foreheads together and breathed each other's air for a moment as Nehami and VanGuard flicked their Y-coms and read off their numbers.

"Fifty-one, sir," said VanGuard.

"Seventy-nine, sir," reported Nehami.

"Good enough. Utenda, you up for some vertical pursuit? VanGuard, down and out. Flank him. I'm resting at twelve percent. I'll anchor." He handed the still-sleeping girl off to her mother. "I'll anchor. Sync in three, two, one, sync." All three double-tapped the insides of their left wrists, where the unique military sensors were located for their Y-coms. All their comms systems came online, as well as their unit tracers, with Mykos as Team Lead. They could talk to each other, keep track of everyone's energy levels and where everyone was in real time.

"Utenda, go. VanGuard, go."

Nehami hopped on the bed and clambered head first out the open window. She kept her grip light, pulling her torso and legs through the narrow opening. She twisted her body around to find hand- and footholds. As far as she could tell, the thief's only enhancements were his eyes, but he had a wiry, resilient strength. He was two stories down already, making steady progress. In another minute, he would be close enough to possibly jump to the ground.

She was going to lose him if she didn't burn some juice. *Conserve*, she thought to herself. *Economy of motion.* The efficiency mantras were some of the few bits of their adaptive rehab therapy that weren't completely useless. Relaxing the rest of her limbs, she used her bioware arm to swing neatly down to the next window ledge. As soon as her toes touched, she let go with her inhumanly strong fingers and crouched into a deep squat before resting the left hand on the ledge between her toes. Again she dropped down, letting her strong arm catch all of her body weight effortlessly until her toes had purchase, fingers curled over the tempered plastic rim.

She did this again and again, getting into a rhythm. Before long, she was only one story up, and she turned to see the thief landing on the ground. He slammed into the pavement, nearly tripping before he took off in a sprint. Resisting the urge to jump, she swung down on her strong arm once more until her feet had purchase on the pavement. A quick glance at her forearm display revealed that VanGuard's avatar was showing higher elevation, still inside the building.

"He's running. Hustle up, V.G."

Whatever they spoke under audible volume was translated by sensors on the high collars that molded organically around their throats. The subvocalizations were translated to vocals directly to the self-repairing nano-mic matrices in their ear canals. They could hear each other as if in the same room, just like when they all talked after lights out, separated by hospital curtains.

"I'll be right behind you," he said.

"This asshole is fast," she complained as she sprinted after the spy.

"Be faster," said Sergeant Mykos, rather unhelpfully. "I'll bet anything he was recording us. I was coming to at the end, and my network sensors went off. His ocular grafts are the same tech as ours, so if they sent him, they know you both broke your NDAs. Do you have him yet?"

"No, sir. Working on it."

Nehami caught her stride, thighs and calves warming, joints pistoning, and arms swinging. He was taller, had longer limbs, but she could see that he was flagging. The rangy Asian man seemed like he'd been running on empty for longer than he could sustain, but he was nimble enough to pivot abruptly and dodge down a side alley between two buildings.

"Coming up on your six, Utenda," said VanGuard.

"Go around. Cut him off at the alley, V.G."

"Will do," he responded.

"Watch out for weapons. Team Lead initiating Trig-jammers. Stand by for a jolt." Sergeant Mykos triggered the triangulation jammer that bounced off each of their iTeegs, making it nearly impossible for signals on most frequencies to be sent within a close radius. It always felt like a jolt of electricity when it initiated. Not very pleasant.

Nehami turned the corner, dragging her living hand on the faux brick texture of the prefab exterior walls to swing herself into the narrow space. There was no one in front of her. She scanned quickly, left and right, and then looked up. Bracing his arms and then his legs, the thief was working his way up toward the top of the building.

"V.G. look up when you get here. Looks like we're going to

be climbing."

VanGuard came around the corner at the other end and looked up.

"Goddamn it," he said.

"Let's go, asteroid slag. Bet I can beat you up dive," challenged Nehami.

"Minimal chatter, corporals. Eyes on the prize."

"Yessir," they both answered as they both took leaping jumps and wedged themselves between the narrowly-spaced buildings to shimmy upward. Nehami was able to brace her legs comfortably, but VanGuard's limbs were long enough to make him bend one knee more than the other, with his elbows and wrists at acute angles. They stuck their feet, moved their arms up, locked their arms and shoulders with palms pressed against exterior walls, and repeated, climbing up at a quick pace. Meanwhile the thief neared the top of the three-story building and hooked his hands over the roof ledge.

"Utenda, you're at forty-five and falling. VanGuard, you're at twenty-two—scratch that—twenty even, and you're going to have to pull back soon."

"Yes, Sergeant. Utenda, meet me in the middle."

VanGuard started working his way toward Nehami. She braced herself and scooted toward him until they were next to each other.

"What are you thinking?"

He took a moment to set his feet and lock his legs hard.

Then he put his hands together, palms up, and looked at her expectantly.

"Want a lift?"

"On three?"

She put one foot and then the other onto his cupped palms, grabbing onto his shoulders. Her knees were bent, and she was crouched down.

"One." They felt out their balance and bounced with it a little.

"Two." Nehami centered herself, and let the potential kinetic energy build up in her legs and hips.

"Three!" As she felt his bioware arms tense and spring upward, she uncoiled and pushed off his lifting hands. The alley became a blur, and, like reaching new heights on a big trampoline, Nehami soared upward. It was terrifying and exhilarating. The atmo-dome loomed closer above until she reached the apex of her arc and started feeling the pull of the artificial gravity. Before it could take her too far, she latched onto the top of the roof to her left, and swung her whole body onto the roof.

"What the hell are you doing, VanGuard? You just dropped from twenty to fourteen percent. Stand down. Utenda, continue pursuit."

"On it," she answered. The man was only a few yards in front of her now. He was stumbling. Nehami put on a burst of speed and tackled him, mid-torso, slamming him into the soft green engineered moss that covered all the buildings.

They rolled awkwardly, elbows flying into cheekbones, limbs twisting. He grunted. She tried to lock around his limbs, and he arched before she could get a joint lock on his arm. He managed to leverage his body, heaving both their weight until he was on his hands and knees. Still wrapped around him, Nehami lunged and looped an arm around his neck. He ducked his chin and got his face in the way before she could close off his air and blood.

She pushed her left arm into his face, mashing his nose down and covering his mouth. Teeth bit into her bioware bicep, but the genetically cloned flesh was interlaced with billion-dollar polymers. It hurt, but it was a distant pain, owing to her low graft integration scores. She persisted. He needed to breathe, so he gave up. His neck arched back, face rising in a desperate bid for air, lips dragging against her cybernetic skin.

He got one ragged gasp. Then she contracted her muscles and, as gently as she could, squeezed his neck and held steady. She felt like she was a toddler, holding a baby bird in her chubby fist. Her heart pounded with adrenaline, and the half a minute it took for the man to go completely limp seemed much longer. As soon as the tension bled from his limbs and tall frame, she let go and pulled the special paracord lengths out of her iTeeg pocket near the right ankle.

"I got him. Sleeper hold. He should be conscious again

soon, unless I overdid it," she reported. "Securing him now."

She tied his elbows together behind his back and wrapped his ankles together, securing the feet to the elbows. All the while, a bitterness coated her tongue.

"Copy that. Good work. Check for a pulse. VanGuard and I are en route."

Nehami swiped at her Y-com and looked at her energy level. Ten percent, falling to nine. Trembling, she scooted on her butt closer to the limp, bound figure. With her living hand, she reached out to check his pulse. It beat steadily. She sighed in relief and let herself fall back onto the roof mosses, chest heaving.

Less than twenty-four hours had passed since she'd stepped off the transport onto her home station, and at this point, being poked and prodded at the lab seemed like a pretty stable assignment by comparison. Expecting that he should have already come to, she glanced back to the man's face. He was clean-shaven, with a good strong jaw. He looked at least ten years younger asleep, and the shadows under his eyes and under his cheekbones made it apparent that there was something wrong.

From the moment he realized he'd been spotted on the other side of the window, he'd displayed none of the swagger and confidence that had oozed from his pores in their earlier interaction. Who he was and what was wrong with him occupied her thoughts at the moment more than why he'd been spying on them. Perhaps he'd shadowed her.

She leaned in cautiously, reaching out to pat the pockets on his coat. They crinkled. She reached in and pulled out dozens of empty snack wrappers, no, not snacks: high-density full-nutrient bars, military grade with expired military labels. But the labels were from the wrong government. Instead of the United Federation of Planetary Nations logo, with a stylized eagle embracing a nebula on an olive-green background, the wrappers displayed three interlocked silver rings raised against a blue background of stars.

Nehami felt her heart rate kick back up a few notches. These bars were military contraband from The Vale, the other side of the long-standing interplanetary war. Either he'd obtained these through the black market or he was directly connected to the Elites.

Nehami shifted the paracord so it wasn't pressing on the Y-com clasped over his wrist. It was scarred and scraped up (probably issued before the upgrade with self-healing nanites), but it was definitely military issue, like her own. What she really wanted to see was the ident-tats on the inner wrist covered by his Y-com. Pulling on the band, she moved it out of the way, revealing a familiar block of dots and lines embedded into skin. She tapped her own Y-com three times in quick succession and scanned his ident-tats.

The holo screen popped up, revealing a low-quality 3D of a very young Asian child. She looked at the unconscious man. It was obviously the same person, but no one gets military ident-tats before they're legally allowed to enter military service at sixteen. Confused, she swiped, highlighting basic information and several case files.

Then she read the file headings. His R-gen coding. He was from the same batch as her, which meant that The Vale owned every aspect of their genetic existence. This guy, like her, had been born on the other side of the conflict. Not even the Lazarus crew knew what lengths she'd gone through to defect, erase her past, and insert herself into the UNFP. Her parents had died to get her out, and she'd nearly died in action saving soldiers who would have shot her if they'd known she was born a designer slave created by the Elites.

"Guys, things just got a lot more complicated ..." she said into the coms. "Sarge, we've got a potential shitstorm. He's a spy for the other side, which means he may have already told them about Lazarus. About us." The truth was that Lazarus wasn't the Federation's project. The faulty but functional bioware grafts that kept them all alive had been reverse-engineered from stolen Vale tech, an attempt to gain traction in the war.

The silence on coms from the team was loaded. Though the tech filtered out breathing and incidental noises, Nehami imagined their sharp inhalations.

"We're almost there. Maintain the jammers, and turn off coms," replied Sergeant Mykos.

She swiped the air and dismissed the holo. Close to her limit, running on fading adrenaline, she sat beside the still form of the mysterious thief. She felt as if she were teetering on the edge of a vast, dark chasm.

Aside from some flimsy clues, the only way she could know the thief was an Elite's designer slave from his R-gen coding was because she knew things that this version of her, a UNFP lifer, could never explain.

It was time to come clean.

Ars Kinetica

by Colin Stricklin

THE WOMAN IN the forest has a large number 19 taped to her back. Her eyes are on the path ahead, and her mind is dodging stones and roots three steps ahead of her feet. She's long-legged, dark-haired and dark-eyed, every part of her pitched to a focus. She's running flat out in front of the pack. The leaders are just ahead.

Rock formations resolve themselves out of twilight. The forest and the runner are on top of a mountain, and the mountain is losing light in a hurry. The runner, number 19, glides along the trail. She lifts her knees and plants her feet, and the ground falls away a piece at a time, a deer's stride and a raptor's face.

Her lungs are burning.

My lungs are fine.

Her left quad threatens to cramp.

My leg feels great.

The cold air is a razor blade in her throat.

Just out for a Sunday stroll.

She grits her teeth and she keeps on pumping. There's a bottleneck coming, a series of boulders hard up to a cliff face. There are 90-degree turns in there, the last tough obstacle, the crankshaft before the home stretch.

She vanishes into the crevice. It's already night inside, ten degrees cooler and dark as an alleyway. But there are echoes too: the front runners coming out the other side.

The first turn screams up out of darkness. She jumps, plants her right foot on a wall, and pushes. The corner goes past and she still has her momentum. Her eyes are wide, staring into the shadows, straining to see the next bend before it's on top of her. Jump, kick, around. She can hear the footsteps. She can smell blood, can picture the finish line and the stopwatch, wants this one so bad, so damned *bad*—

Corner.

Jump.

Kick.

But the last wall is slippery and a boulder slams against an elbow.

Falling.

She hits the ground hard, and the grit of the trail is like sandpaper. She curses through her teeth.

The elbow is a dull throb at her side.

My arm is fine.

Her left knee hurts worse than the arm.

My knee is perfect.

She does a quick push-up and stands. She growls, hops a little on the right leg, tests the left, and keeps on. She can see the light of the parking lot through the trees below, the finish line. She can still hear the footsteps from downhill. The light and the sound and the nearness of the end get her legs back to speed. She can still do this thing. The downhill is her strength; she can take the hairpins at a skid and make up ground. She'll have to.

Her dark eyes are full from wanting it. Her pace is picking up again, though her stride is no longer fluid. She isn't flowing and leaping now, but *pounding* down the mountain, her body protesting all the way.

The first switchback, taking it low, back hand trailing the dirt for balance, pebbles rolling beneath her shoes. Around and back out, a few steps at full speed, drop to the sliding crouch.

Again.

Again.

Again.

And now she can hear the up-ahead breathing. She can hear the first of the leaders and *knows* that she will pass. There's plenty left in the tank. There's plenty of time. Just one more hairpin, a quarter-mile sprint, and then bright lights and cups of Gatorade. There's victory down there, exaltation.

"Rock!"

Her priorities shift. There's a sound like thunder from

uphill and behind. A sound like plate tectonics.

"Rock!" cries the voice again. "Rock rock rock!"

And she tries to hold up, tries to do what she's been taught and dive for the retaining wall. But her left leg seizes. It does not bend. And runner number 19 is standing straight as a bowling pin when the world explodes into white.

OPENING HER EYES, groggy at first. Everything is still white.

This light doesn't burn though. It doesn't break. It's a color like cotton swabs, or disinfectant, or clean gauze across a wound. There's a ditto sheet clipped to the foot of her bed. It says *Mary Anne Knudsen. 28. F. Spiral fracture of the right femur. Left tibia and fibula crushed. Displaced trimalleolar fractures in left foot.*

And the list goes on. Mary can't read these things. She's lying on her back on the bed, and the paper is out of sight. Her legs are suspended in casts and slings with counterweights. The pain is a dull black throb even through the medication.

Mary remembers and she groans. At the bottom of the slope, the leaders just ahead and the pack coming out of the crankshaft behind. Someone must have put a foot down. A piece of granite must have come loose, shifted just enough, and begun to roll. By the bottom of the hill, by the time it met Mary, it was rolling too fast to dodge.

Mary remembers these things. And looking at her plastered legs suspended like so much deli meat, she *gets* it. So how is it fair that she should have to lie back and hear? Tom, her coach, is whispering with the doctor. They're using the worst sorts of words, words like *"intensive"* and *"reconstruction"*. And when the subject of Mary's trail running comes up, she hears shuffling feet and mumbled condolences. She hears Tom swear beneath his breath. But the important word, the only one that really matters, is *"never"*.

And that doesn't seem fair at all.

THE WOMAN IN the doorway is holding an enormous purse and a vase of gift-shop flowers.

"Mary? Are you doing okay? Are you up for a little visit? I can just let myself out if you're tired …?"

"Hi Mom," rasps Mary. "Water?"

The vase clicks down onto a bedside table, disappearing into the rest of the jungle. Miniature greeting cards hidden in the foliage say things like "from the team" and "your coach misses you" and "we regret to inform you we're dropping your sponsorship." A glass of water emerges from the leaves.

Mary drinks. Sighs. "Thanks Mom. How do I look?"

"Wonderful, honey. You look better every day." There's dampness in her eyes though. Her smile wavers as she perches her skinny frame on the end of the chair. "Do you want to borrow some moisturizer? I've got it in here someplace." She rummages in the purse, a woven hemp monster of a bag, and Mary imagines a sparrow scratching for seeds.

"Aha!" The elder Knudsen emerges from the depths of her bag. "It's banana-scented. Is that okay?"

Mary leans over to take the bottle. She winces as her legs sway in traction. "Thanks," she says, spreading the lotion. She winces again. It really is banana-scented.

"So," says Patty Knudsen, "how are you bearing up?"

"Oh, I'm keeping myself entertained. There's thirty-two channels on the TV and a copy of **Family Circus** somewhere under the flowers. Honestly, it's thrilling to the point of overstimulation. Thank God there's a morphine button." Mary tries a wry smile, but it only comes out miserable.

"Oh, honey. I'm so sorry. The doctor says you can't run anymore but what do doctors know? Because here, look." Patty begins to hunt and peck through the purse again. "I went to the store earlier and I found some things that might help." A pile of objects begins to accumulate on the foot of Mary's bed. There are crystals at its base. Then a layer of audio tapes appears along with an ancient yellow Walkman. There's a candle. There are copper bracelets. A color wheel. And finally, a top layer of books with titles like **The Psychic Energy Workbook** and **Healing Chi** and **The Spiritual MD**.

"I didn't know what to get, so I got everything."

Patty Rainbow Starshine Knudsen sniffs loudly and dabs at

her eyes. "I know how much the competition means to you. And you really are good at it, and I would so love to see you happy and doing what you love outdoors and out of this horrible hospital. I,"

(sniff. honk)

"I don't know if any of it will do any good. Except the aromatherapy candle. That always makes me feel better. But it can't do any harm, right? And maybe it will be better than the TV and the tatty magazines. Please say you'll try, honey. Okay?"

And now it is Mary's turn to blink back tears.

"Thank you Mom," she says and holds open her arms for the hug. She doesn't believe in any of it. She actually hates that her mother wasted the money, but it is still a gesture that is more interesting than flowers. She grits her teeth when the embrace nudges her leg.

✦   ✦   ✦

	Mary		up		Get		Mary
up		Get		Mary		up	
	Mary		up		Get		
up		Get		Mary			Get
Get		Mary		smiles		up	Mary
	Mary		up		Get		Mary
up		Get		Mary		up	

✦　　✦　　✦

SHE'S ALWAYS IN doctors' offices now, assigning numbers to her pain level, trying to wiggle her toes.

"Very good. And one more time."

Mary says, "Okay," between gritted teeth.

Then she staggers. She clutches at the parallel bar, re-balances, and takes another step. She remembers a movie from her childhood, some version of **Black Beauty**, the foal with its first horseshoes trying to run and the hooves kicking out, unwieldy.

Mary's knees barely bend. It's like walking on stilts.

"And ... time. Three laps in 47.09 seconds. How do you feel?"

"Tired."

It is the truth. Hobbling around her apartment is bad enough, but, without the crutches or even the cane, the short trips along the parallel bars feel like wind sprints.

The therapist smiles his grad-student smile and says, "You're getting better."

"Sure. I move like the goddamn wind, don't I?"

His smile becomes forced. He breaks eye contact and pre-tends to jot on the clipboard. The tests proceed, all par for the course, all business as usual now.

Mary wheezes. Human figures fill up the space of the PT gym, all moving through stretches and contortions and specialized lifts. Some of these figures are athletes. Some of the athletes are men, and so remind Mary of Tom.

"We were driven," he'd said. "Both of us. That's what made us work."

He'd finally mustered enough courage to end things yesterday. He'd been the last piece of her life as a runner.

"Now let's try counterclockwise," says the therapist.

"As far as you can."

"I'm going to push. Tell me when to stop."

Eventually Mary makes a copay. She leans against the desk while she signs.

"Same time next week?" The receptionist's face is bright and perky. Mary wants to smash it with her crutch.

"You know it," she says. It even sounds normal in her own ears.

Out to the car then, an unnatural tripod-person sort of walk, and then the crutches are stored and the seat is adjusted and she drives herself home.

IT HAD BEEN a full month before the hospital let her go. Returning to her apartment, feeding kibble to Toby, smelling the familiar musk of her own closet and bed had all felt almost normal. So had the visit from Tom. *How are you holding up? We're all thinking about you. Listen, we have to talk.* You could barely notice the tightness around his mouth. It was hard to spot his eyes, unsympathetic flecks of green, flicking to the metal mangle of her legs.

Mary's workouts no longer involve weights. Certainly they no longer involve going outside. It is TheraBands and stretching routines for her. Climbing stairs? Doable, but hey, that's what the cripple ramp is there for. Getting up to answer the phone? Getting out of bed in the morning? Going to the mailbox? Going to the goddamn bathroom? Everything is embarrassing. Everything is awful.

And the insurance money will run out soon. Just like the sympathy cards. Just like the calls from her teammates. Not to mention the calls from her sponsors, though she doesn't need those now. They had only ever given equipment. And running shoes are not a priority. Fresh rags on the crutches are a priority. Medications are priority. Therapy instead of training. Hobbling instead of running. And now Mary drifts where before she strode. Mary stops at a red light.

The smell of exhaust leaks in on her. She coughs. Her foot falls off the pedal.

"Oh no."

And of course the light turns green before she can reset. The left lane, the fast lane, is accelerating past. Any second now, the drivers behind her will begin to lean on their horns. She's near tears as her hands grip at her pant leg, trying to reposition, just trying to get home.

"You can't do anything," she says. "You're stupid. I hate

you. Please, damn it. Please."

And her foot manages to find the pedal. She heads through the intersection, embarrassed and in pain, and hears the car horns behind her, irritated and unkind. She speeds all the way home. She doesn't feel like she's moving at all.

"TOBY. I'M HOME."

The beagle's sharp little claws click across the linoleum. "Arf," he says, and does not jump up on Mary. He used to, and Mary had always encouraged him. *I'm happy to see you too. Who gives kisses? Do you give puppy kisses?* But retraining had been necessarily quick. He'd hit the stitches with his feet, and that had been that. So now he squirms on his haunches at her feet, and he grins up at her and licks his lips.

"Did you miss me?"

He turns a circle and sits again.

Mary laughs. "I'll get the can opener." The beagle follows along behind, looking up with enormous eyes and bright white teeth. He's broadcasting hunger and love in equal measure, and it is a tonic to Mary's shattered nerves. The honest point of his brown and white face is just the same as ever. Dogs, Mary reflects, do not change. They have integrity.

Toby whines impatiently while Mary turns the crank. He licks his chops as she gets the bowl. His nose twitches as she bends slowly, painfully down to the ground with his food.

Mary is panting a bit when she says, "Good boy," and straightens.

She watches her dog eat for a few moments, tries to smile at his simple happiness, fails, and begins to walk to the living room. Her television is in there, and, as much as she'd rather not, TV is the one thing that really *is* easy.

She creaks her way painfully down onto the couch. She flips around and settles on a channel and leans back. Once upon a time she made fun of people like this, the sad slobs who got home from work and plopped down and stared at a stupid screen.

BURRRRRING!

Mary stares at the jacket on the kitchen table. Another easy thing ruined. She stands too slowly, walks too slowly, and gets to the jacket pocket too late.

Menu > Missed Calls > Mom > Send

"Mary Anne? Is that you?"

"Yeah Mom. What's up?"

"You told me you would keep a cell phone with you all the time. Where are you? Are you okay?"

"It's okay Mom. You just caught me doing my exercises, that's all." Mary's eyes flick towards her therapy bands. She has been doing her exercises. Most nights. When she feels motivated.

"Oh. Well that's alright then. But Mary, are you doing *all* your exercises?" Her mother hasn't stopped talking about the New Age remedies. Without much else for a pastime, Mary has been happy enough to give them a try. But as each successive technique has failed, it's become harder and harder to humor her mother's hippy streak.

Nevertheless she says, "Yes Mom. The **Ascended Masters** CD is great. I'm centering myself three times a day now."

"Oh. You're still using that one? I always thought it was a bit silly."

Mary breathes a sigh of relief. The pile of remedies is getting smaller. Soon she will be able to say *Nothing did the trick. It was a nice try and we gave it our best, but I think I'll just stick to the physical therapy.*

"No," says Patty. "If we're really going to tap into your energies, you should focus on **Nightlife**. You've been keeping your dream journal, right?"

"Yes, Mom. I keep it next to my bed."

"And …?"

"My dreams have been getting more vivid," she admits. "At least the book is right about that." The book in question, **Nightlife: A Roadmap to the Astral Plane**, also promises out-of-body experiences, spirit guides, and journeys to higher planes of reality. The illustrations of translucent figures floating serenely through the cosmos are not especially convincing.

"Oh honey, I know how it sounds. But it's only silly if you look at things logically. You've got to have a bit of faith. And it doesn't hurt to try."

Mary tries not to sigh. She fails. "Sure Mom. I'll stick with it." She tries to inject a little optimism into her tone and says, "You never know."

There's a pause on the other end of the line. Mary can imagine her mother's worried face, lower lip bitten and eyes anxious. "Honey, I don't know if it will help. But I tried it once and the lucid dreaming was fun and it's *something*, you know?"

"I'll try it Mom. It's not like I'm doing much else."

✦   ✦   ✦

	with	me	Come	me
Come	with	me	with
	Come	me	Come
me	with	me	Come
with	Come	all smiles here	with	me
me	with	Come	me
with	Come	me	with
Mary	with	Come
with	Come	me	Come
Come	me	with	me

✦ ✦ ✦

MARY IS RESTED and refreshed. She is at the farmer's market with her mother, and the cane is all she needs today. Her grip is strong and her smile is easy.

"What about oregano, Ms. Secret Sauce?"

"No oregano," says the elder Knudsen.

"Heresy!"

The mother and daughter laugh easily. It is cooking night for them, a lifelong once-a-week affair. It's Patty's turn. She's doing Italian.

"Bell peppers?"

"Nope."

"Onions?"

"Uh-uh."

"At least tell me there's garlic."

"Wrong again."

"What!"

"OK. Maybe we'll buy garlic."

They laugh again. They buy the produce. Return home. Simmer for several hours. Enjoy the seafood risotto. Bid each other good night.

Mary feels happy. But in her bed, with the negative space that Coach Thomas Michelson has left behind, the happiness ebbs away. She shuts her eyes, tries to relax, and wishes there was more in her life than her mother and the warm lump of dog at her side. She attempts to breathe deeply, to enter something called a 'hypnagogic state.' Find a comfortable position, then focus on something small: a finger or a toe. Try to move it with your mind.

Mary is unconscious when she enters a state of extraplanar vibration, so she's not aware of the ripples that spread from her mind, or the attention that they draw.

✦   ✦   ✦

You've   a   greater   vibrate
at   You've   got   to
        frequency   at   vibrate
    got   greater   You've   a
frequency   vibrate can't you hear me?   to
        You've   a   frequency
to   greater   at   got
    vibrate   a   frequency   at
        You've   got   to
    vibrate   at   a   greater
frequency   got   vibrate   to

✦   ✦   ✦

TOBY, PRESSED CLOSE against a gnarled chunk of his owner's thigh, is running in his sleep. His little paws thrash at the sheets, at the darkness, and at the fragrant earth of the dreamland.

They're still his paws. He is still himself, a brown-white mass of house pet hurtling through underbrush and pine needles. He's also far larger. He's faster, and his ears are shaped differently, and his stumpy legs push him at impossible speed between the trees and after the squirrel.

Its thick brush of tail is always just out of reach. It's always flashing in a new direction, down a gully and over a bank, but Toby is too close this time. He is too near for the little morsel of fur and irritation to take to the trees. He will catch it if it tries, and the rest of the pack, the ones running just behind, will see. They will grin feral grins as he thrashes his head and the sweet hot taste of meat pours between his teeth and down his throat.

It is the best dream possible.

It is vibrant. It is bright and perfect. It is everything a little dog could ever want, right up until the moment the world begins to quake. The fabric of the dreamland, the fabric of Toby's brown and white consciousness, begins to break and fall. The smell of the squirrel is burning. It is acrid and almonds and a pain in his nose. Colors that are neither black nor white flash through the forest, and they're unfamiliar and impossible to his canine sensorium. And now it's not the pack that's chasing Toby. It's a thing with only two legs. And it's reaching, and its hands are black, and it's nothing like a dog. Or a wolf. Or a human being. Nothing at all.

On the other side of the bed, Mary sleeps on. She does not

perceive the movements of her dog. Not even when they grow frantic. Not even when they shudder to a stop.

She does not perceive the thing leaning over her bed.

✦　　✦　　✦

THERE IS A tree in the garden behind Patty Rainbow Starshine Knudsen's house. It is a magnolia, and its leaves are glossy green. Its blossoms are sweet-smelling on the summer air. And beneath its canopy, the leaf litter is raked away.

"Hi Dad," says Mary. She's looking at the little circle of stones and the little wreath of flowers beside the trunk. Her father's ashes are beneath them.

"Do you think about him often?" asks Patty.

Mary nods. She wipes at her eye with the back of her hand. "I remember his shoes in the hallway. The blue Nikes. Mine always looked small beside them."

Patty puts her arm around her daughter's shoulders.

"I miss him too." She squeezes Mary's shoulder. "He's got Toby now. They can go for their morning jogs again."

Mary nods. She would speak more, but she doesn't trust her voice. It was a heart attack that got her dad. He had been in great shape, eaten well, run every day, placed in the over-fifties marathons, but it was still a heart attack. It is stupid and unfair, but there it is, just the same.

Pointless.

Tragic.

Blue Nikes in a hallway.

"Okay," says Mary. "Okay." She lets herself fall to her knees while the braces squeak and protest. It hurts. Even against the soft dark earth beneath the magnolia tree, it hurts, but she ignores it. There are gloves on her hands and a spade in her fist. She begins to dig.

Patty joins her, and the hole starts to take shape. It is a little less than three feet long, and, by the time the afternoon fades, it is a little less than three feet deep. There are blisters on Mary's hands, grit in her eyes and mouth. The last of the day's yellow jackets buzz dreamily around the magnolia blossoms. Sunset comes down between the boughs, and green beams of light play all around them.

On the ground at Mary's side is a bundle in an old sheet. It is surprisingly light. Taking it up in her arms, Mary thinks that it's like lifting a gentle breeze. Or a cobweb. Or the wave hello and goodbye of a friend.

"I love you, buddy," says Mary. And now tears start in earnest.

Her mother's arm is on her shoulder, but she does not feel it. She feels deserted. She feels like there's no one left in her world. She starts to scoop loose earth back atop the grave.

The sunset burns its way through the sky, gold and glory and warm summer evening. Out at the road beyond Patty's house the streetlights are kicking on. It's night already beneath the magnolia tree.

✦   ✦   ✦

you   let   me   a   little   you
   already me   in   let   already
let   a   in   little   you   little   already
   let   me   in   a   little
you   me   jet black teeth   over   way
   come   way   the   rest   over   the over
rest   of   come   the   way   the
   over   way   come   rest   of
the   way   over   rest   of   come

✦   ✦   ✦

MARY DOESN'T DO her exercises anymore. Not the physical ones anyway. She is depressed. She knows because her doctors prescribed the very large bottle of antidepressants, and that makes it official.

The dating site did not work out well.

Single white female. No interests. Physically defective.

There hadn't been many responses.

Her first appearance at a meet hadn't gone much better. The other woman, her replacement, had smiled politely. She'd asked politely after her health. And then, just as politely, she'd walked away to stretch or stow her things or just get-the-hell-away from the cripple.

"Hi, Coach."

"Mary!"

"It's a ten-mile, right?"

Tom had opened his mouth, closed it. He'd seen the tightness lining Mary's face.

"That's right." He'd made a show of checking his clipboard. "It's ten point three total. They'll be gaining 900 feet before the end."

"How far do you think I could get?"

"Mary, please don't."

"Don't what? I'm not going to try it. We both know I'm not quite that handy-capable."

Mary's voice had been low and dangerous. It hadn't risen, but there were magma and scorn beneath the surface.

"No worries, Coach. Maybe I'll hang out at the table with the little cups of Gatorade. I'll hand them out to all the real people, and maybe if I'm lucky someone will sweat on me."

Wisely, Michelson hadn't said anything. He'd just watched her walk away, his eyes sad and his nerves seeming stretched.

Now Mary is home, in front of the television, on top of the couch, trying her best to zone out.

She does not want to do anything. She does not want to go anywhere or talk to anyone. She just wants to curl up in a ball and not think about her failed lover and her failed life. She wants the parts of existence between sleeping and sleeping to hurry the hell up.

So her eyes are heavy. So the couch is warm and welcoming. And because it's become a habit, and because she has practiced every night since Patty Rainbow Starshine Knudsen brought her a stack of books, Mary attempts to breathe deeply, to enter a hypnagogic state. She closes her eyes and falls asleep.

But Mary Anne Knudsen is not unconscious.

For a gut-wrenching moment the interior walls of her world try to shake themselves apart. The fabric of her thoughts vibrates at a terrible foreign frequency, and her lungs forget how to draw breath. But then she sits up in bed. She looks around wildly. She puts a steadying hand on the bedside table.

There's nothing there to greet her. No shadows move toward her. It's just her bedroom, dark and quiet. But the weird shaking is fresh and vivid, and she is still just this side of panic. She stands up and calls out, "Hello?"

There is no answer. Just a soft breathing sound at her back. Mary whirls, fists raised, feet spread in a fighter's stance, and looks down at her own sleeping form. Her mouth, her conscious self's mouth, drops open in shock. Her brain doesn't process. Her body stalls in place.

In a moment, the conclusions will all rush in at once. *Mom was right. I'm dreaming.*

But for now she leans over the bed and sees familiar strands of brunette hair sweat-plastered to her other self's cheek. The too-thin face is frowning slightly, and the eyes move like birds' heads, twitching frenetically beneath their lids.

Aloud Mary says, "I look like shit," and she laughs. Then her eyes move down the length of blanket. One pale knee is poking out. It's plastic in appearance and deeply scarred, and almost immediately the depression returns.

Mary repeats, "I look like shit," and she takes a step back from herself. Then her eyes go wide again. She takes another step back. And another. She crouches low and then jumps in place, and her head brushes against the ceiling.

THE WOMAN IN the forest has a large number 19 taped to her back. The book calls this *residual self-image*. She thinks of herself as an athlete, so she looks like an athlete. Her eyes are on the path ahead, and her mind is electric bright. Beneath the night-black trees and the distant stars, she seems more vivid, more real, than everything else. Her legs are long again, tight-muscled and sleek. Her hair is flowing and her eyes are dark, and every part of her is pitched to a focus. She's running flat out by herself in the dark. She's on a familiar track.

Into the crevice one more time, and it's like a camera strapped to a rollercoaster, to a jet fighter. She's moving too fast to perceive the turns. *CornerJumpKickCornerJumpKick* and through. The switchbacks and the downhill, and there's no rock to stop her this time. There is nothing to stop her, and the last quarter-mile of straightaway is a few fast strides.

Mary raises her arms at the stars and breathes hard and

grins. It's better than it's ever been. It hardly matters that she's the only one running. It hardly matters that she didn't really win anything.

NIGHTS COMPOUND. MARY becomes faster. Stronger. Her body's muscles slacken.

When she's awake, her mother comments on this. "Honey, are you feeling alright?"

"Absolutely." Mary's voice is low and whispery, but her lips are wrenched into a smile.

"Well, if you say so. I worry about you."

"You don't need to. I feel great. Better than great. I've never been better. I'm going to take a nap."

Patty watches her daughter limp away. She thinks about old friends, wild-eyed junkies that died or dropped out of touch a thousand years back. She remembers seizures and bad trips and frantic ambulance rides, so she can't help but worry about her emaciated daughter. Vicodin maybe? Probably.

Patty closes her eyes and rubs her temples and tries to soothe her mind. The breathing exercises don't work. Neither does the incense when she gets home. Neither does sleeping on it.

MARY SHUTS HER eyes and adjusts her frequency. She doesn't

spare a glance for her sleeping self.

It's into the woods. It's a quick warm-up run around the old course, and then on to more exotic locales. She can go anywhere now. Maybe Nepal tonight, straight up the side of Everest. She begins to stretch.

Something moves. Her eyes lock onto the shadow thing in the trees.

"hello   hi   Mary hi   hi   hello
Mary   hello hi   hello Mary hello"

Mary straightens again. She does not take her gaze from the shadow thing. Its mouth moves and words come piping out of it, but she does not hear them. Not really. She feels them, and it is not a pleasant sensation. She takes an involuntary step backwards.

"Hello," she says.

The thing hasn't moved. It doesn't seem to have any eyes, but they're looking at her anyway.

"to   try   adjust   try   you   I'll
adjust   to   I'll   you   to   try"

"Excuse me?" says Mary. She blinks her eyes and rubs at them as the thing refocuses.

"I said, my very dear Mary, that I will attempt to adjust to you. It would appear that I've succeeded."

The thing has a voice like silk and broken glass. It literally hurts to hear.

"I seldom have to adjust downwards. I confess that it's a unique and not entirely disagreeable sensation. A bit of an ego boost, you see."

Mary is getting over the fear in a hurry. Anger is replacing it. "What are you doing in my dream?" she says.

"It would seem that I'm insulting you."

"And can you explain to me why I shouldn't just throw you out?"

The laughter is terrible, but Mary grits her teeth and bears it. The thing says, "By all means, try."

Mary tries. She pushes hard at the fabric of the world that she still thinks of as a dream, and the trees around the creature seem to heat-shimmer and twist. The thing is still sharp though. It's still there. Its overlong fingers brush imaginary dust from an imaginary sleeve.

"My but that was amusing, wasn't it? Would you care to try again? I'd love for you to exhaust yourself."

Mary shakes her head. She is panting. "What are you?" she says.

"Ah, precisely the question. Precisely."

Mary is still trying to get her breath back.

"How far," says the thing, "did you get in your mother's book?"

"How did you—"

The thing lifts a hand. "Indulge me."

"I only ever skimmed it. Just the step by step bits."

"So none of the theory?"

Mary blinks. "I guess not."

"Then you know nothing of the creatures that share this plane?"

"No," says Mary.

"You didn't even read up on the basic charms?"

"No."

"My, my, my. It *was* a cursory look on your part, wasn't it? Every starry-eyed high schooler with a smattering of Wicca seems to pick up a ward or two. But not you, Mary. You were just desperate enough to make it through. You were just dumb enough to come unprepared."

The thing flows towards Mary. The mask of its face is a jagged blank, but Mary can tell that it's wearing a smile. She gets the feeling that there are teeth inside of it.

"I've been watching and listening, Mary. I've been at your bedside. Couldn't you hear me? Couldn't you feel me?"

The thing reaches a hand out, perversely gentle, for Mary's face. She makes her break. She's dashing for the tree line, for the old foot path she knows so well. She skids to a stop when the creature bars her way.

"You *are* a quick one. Much faster than that sad little dog of yours."

Mary's nostrils flare. Her fists clench.

"Poor Toby. Why, he was hardly even a mouthful." The terrible laughter again.

Mary punches towards it, teeth gritted and dark eyes alight, but there's nothing there to hit. The featureless black shape, the shadow, simply flows around her fist.

"easy   dodge another   plane to   easy
dodge   on   plane   to   easy   another"

Mary glares at the shape as it reforms.

"Now Mary, I'm afraid that wasn't very ladylike. Such a savage little jock girl." It makes a *tsk tsk* sort of sound, shaking its head. "I am, however, willing to give you another chance to play nice. Don't you want to play nice with me?"

Mary spits at the shape.

"Pearls before humans. And here I was, willing to challenge you to an honest footrace."

Warily Mary says, "Footrace?"

"Oh, now I see that I've got your attention. You really do have a narrow focus in life. You ought to broaden your horizons a bit."

If it's possible, Mary's glare deepens. The thing only laughs.

"The rules are simple enough, even for one such as you, my dear. It's a straight shot out to Alpha Centauri. One lap and back again. First one back to your body wins."

Mary turns her gaze skywards. *Alpha Centauri …*

The thing is standing beside her. It's looking upwards too, a "hand" over its "eyes" in parody of Mary's posture.

"Why?" she says.

"Why what? The race? Don't you like to play with your food?"

Mary makes a conscious effort to keep from shuddering. "And what are the stakes?" she says. "I assume that you want to eat me or my soul or whatever, but what do I get?"

"Oh you are very much mistaken, Mary. We're both racing for the same thing, possession of a corporeal body. *Your* corporeal body."

Mary's eyes go wide. The thing seems not to notice.

"I suppose," it says, "that I *could* eat your psyche as easily as poor little Toby's. But where's the fun in that? It's far better to take your flesh for my own. Think of the havoc I could wreak."

Mary swallows. She tries to remain calm, but malice is sheeting off the thing like rainwater from a windshield. It's repulsive. It's difficult to keep from bolting. "Which way," says Mary, "to Alpha Centauri?"

The thing makes a noise somewhere between amusement and disgust. It points to a pinpoint of light in the eastern sky.

"One two three go," it says.

"What?"

But the creature is already gone.

THE WOMAN IN the forest, number 19, is about to crash into a tree. She's never run upwards before (it was tough enough to run on water the first time). She needs a psychological push. So she thinks of old cartoons, of rabbits and roosters with legs blurring to circles, running straight up the sides of things.

She leaps.

Her feet find purchase on the bark, and her astral self approaches the vertical. The branches pass around her. The canopy screams down towards her, and the toe-tip of one white Nike catapults from the crown.

Earth falls away.

For one mote of time there's dusky sky and whipped white clouds, but that's gone in a hurry.

Ionosphere

Magnetosphere.

Sol fading in the rear view of her

consciousness.

She cannot see the shadow, but she can feel him. He's hurtling like a night-black comet through the darker color of the void. Out through the Oort cloud now and into interstellar proper, Mary follows the dark thread spooling out ahead of her. She's getting closer. The shadow's fraction of a light year head start is shrinking, the parallax shift of its flight becoming more pronounced with proximity. The light of a pinpoint, Alpha Centauri, flickers with it. Even now it's getting brighter.

An interstellar body in the space between interstellar bodies, Mary surpasses the speed of light.

Her self is burning.

My ego is fine.

Her left frontal lobe threatens to cramp.

My brain feels great.

The cold of space is a numbness around her mind.

Just out for a Sunday stroll.

There are grain-of-sand-sized bits of dust out here. Mary weaves around them, her consciousness like radar a hundred million miles ahead of her course. It's been bare seconds since Earth, and already the disk of the alien star is growing large in the sky. It's splitting. It's resolving itself into a second star, a binary pair. It's a shuttle race on a grand scale, and Mary is nearing the turnaround.

The shadow has already made it. He's coming back again. They pass one another with the width of an alien sun between them. They pass inside a unit of time approaching indivisibility.

And Mary is smiling.

Through the magnetic arc of a solar flare, orange and gold in the infinite night. Mary is on the return home.

A missile.

A ray of light.

An angel made of velocity. And the fabric of the plane is reduced to waves and particles as Mary passes through it.

As she passes the swearing, sweating creature.

Sol is a place again rather than a light, and Mary screams toward it. Jupiter is gone in a blink. The moon is too big to dodge, so she simply passes through it. Layers of atmosphere moving around her like rings of fire. And then the roof of her house. And then the threads of her carpet soft upon bare feet.

It has been nearly thirty seconds since the start of the race. Exultant, Mary begins to lower her frequency. She begins to wake up. Her physical eyes begin to flutter.

But the black knife fingers of the shadow's hand close around her throat. Mary is jerked violently back to the astral plane, and there she begins to choke.

"Oh no, Mary," says the thing. "I'm afraid you don't get away."

Mary is flung headlong into the corner of her own bedroom. She manages to slow most of the momentum, but she has to struggle to maintain consciousness. The shadow is walking towards her now. Its teeth and its eyes and its rage are invisible, flat black on flat black, but the impression is there.

"You don't get to win."

Mary tries to stand, but the thing strikes her again. And again.

And the next blow sends Mary halfway into the wall. The shadow looks down at her, panting and wrathful, and Mary spits blood onto the floor. She's smiling, the dark flecks of her eyes pointed insolently upwards.

"Sorry, but it looks like I *did* win. Stupid little me, better and stronger than you. A little girl and a pair of Nikes."

The shadow flinches. It looks around warily, ears cocked

and nostrils flaring. "Shut up," says the thing. "Don't say that."

Mary opens her mouth. She closes it. Thinks for a second. Then slowly and clearly, she says again, "A little girl and a pair of Nikes."

The creature hisses.

A low hum begins to sound through the dim of the bedroom. Mary stands up, and now it's the creature's turn to flinch away.

"Nikes?" she says. And the low hum becomes a tremor.

"No!" says the thing. It dives headlong into the emaciated body on the bed, and the shaking of the world continues.

"Nike," says Mary, feeling like a schoolgirl chanting a taunt. "Nike Nike Nike!"

The entity howls. It is sinking slowly, too slowly, into Mary's body. Its legs are black twigs poking from Mary's pale flesh. The tips of its ears still jut out, dark triangles against the bed sheets as an earthquake rocks the house. As a hole rips its way through the air. As the sound of thunderbolts cascades through.

There's a third figure in the room now. She is blinding. She is beautiful. And her hand is wrapped around the black shadow's ankle.

It thrashes. It screams wordlessly, but it is drawn back out of the body, a charred and loathsome thing. In the merciless light Mary can finally make out its features, the hundred eyes, the scarecrow gash of a mouth, the viscous stuff of its saliva.

"Not fair," it screams. *"Not fair. NOT FAIR!"*

Its needle-teeth gnash upon themselves. Its face contorts in fury and in fear.

But a word is spoken then. It is many syllables long and mellifluous. In later years Mary will try to remember it. She will try to pronounce it herself, to write it, to sing it, but will never quite match timbre or tone. And as the echo of the word passes through her room and her body and her self, the black form of the shadow falls apart. And the pieces fly away, borne on a wind that Mary cannot feel.

Sound fades away. Sensation fades away. For a few moments, in the presence of this star-bright lady, Mary knows only light.

But it does not last. The figure dims a few degrees, and Mary can see now that the lady's standing in a chariot.

Mary, who can think of nothing else, says, "Thank you."

"Of course." The woman is grinning broadly now. "It's only polite to come when called."

Mary struggles to think. There are tears on her face, though she does not know why. "Who are you?"

The figure points at Mary's feet. "You bear the symbol of my wings."

Mary considers this. She says, "You're Nike."

The figure smiles.

"Why did you help me?"

Laughter like bells. "It's not so often that I get to watch

such a contest as the one you just won. Surely that deserves some reward."

Mary nods dumbly. But then her breath catches. Her eyes go wide. "You can heal me. You can fix my legs."

The merriment vanishes from Nike's face. "No Mary. Not in the sense that you mean."

The trail runner lowers her eyes. For a moment the hope had been there, bright and strong. Now she's looking down at the twisted limbs of her other self, and she can feel nothing at all.

"Understand Mary, this is a place of the mind. In your world I cannot move a pebble, much less mend your bones or flesh. But—"

Mary raises her eyes, and a laurel wreath comes down across her brow. The light is once more blinding.

IN THE GRANDSTANDS of a stadium, Patty Rainbow Starshine Knudsen watches her daughter.

It's been a strange transformation these past months. The changes were slow at first. The dark rings had gone from her daughter's eyes. She'd begun to eat well. She'd started back on the PT regimen.

"Mary, dear. Were you ... have you been on something? It was pain killers, wasn't it?"

And her daughter had said, "Yeah Mom. It was pain killers. But don't worry, I've lowered the dosage. I'm using properly now." She had sounded natural and carefree, and Patty had believed her. So for once she hadn't worried.

Mary's legs became stronger. They would never be perfect but they were *better*. First the braces had gone. Then the crutches. And by the time the training started in earnest, she only had to use the cane.

The old hippy's teeth bite hard against her bottom lip, and her thin-boned fists are tight balls in her lap. There are echoes from the concrete walls. There is a cheer from the crowd. And when Patty stands up, when she inhales to shout her encouragement (*Go Mary go!*) her nostrils flair to the smell of chlorine.

In the final length of the final heat, Mary's stroke is nearly flawless. The tight cords of her arms more than make up for the weak kick, and she is neck and neck for the wall.

She is pulling ahead.

She is first.

There are medals. There are congratulations. There is photography and joy and Paralympic pomp. But later on, in an interview, there is a question: "Before the accident, you were a professional-level distance runner. There aren't many athletes who could have made that sort of transition. What was it like retraining for a new sport?"

Mary says, "I just love the competition. It was tough, but when you love something like that, you can't let it go. Besides," and a light comes into Mary's dark eyes, "it feels natural being in the water. You can move in all three dimensions. Like flying. Exactly like flying."

Almost Human
by Lynn Finger

ZOOMING THROUGH A passage of this virtual space station in my favorite game, Throwback, my gaming identity character (GIC) sped like a comet unleashed in zero G. I guided her skillfully, whooping and yelling (to myself, mind you) as she swam the tunnels, twisting and turning throughout the maze like a neutrino looking for an electron to hug. Her black hair flowed out behind her as she made her way through all the little corners and straightaways at a startling speed.

I and my competitors were looking for the treasures hidden on this large cybership, and I had homed in on this section without the pull of centrifugal gravity. It was a challenging game setting, with blind corners everywhere and areas of complete darkness, but I was never bothered by that. My identity was Badreck, and I was just squeaking ahead of two of my opponents, CTpax and Surivam1. Competitor Dubdub2 was a hot one and she was way ahead. I struggled to keep up, catching glimpses of her white coat flying behind her.

The game had started in a gravity-bound part of the virtual

space station, but I quickly went to the zero G section, searching for treasure. I swirled my character through the main hold with the speed of a plasma blob, heading for the lab where the experiments were kept.

We'd been given some clues for this level of the game, and the clue "a box of rain", I suspected, could refer to the lab filters. In real life, space dwellers like me needed vital life support, including the removal of excess water vapor from the air. I didn't know much about how these things worked, but I knew where to locate them.

The red GIC male figure of Surivam1 was blasting right next to me, not falling behind or pulling ahead as we barreled through the passages of our game. Was he following me? And there was Dubdub2! But suddenly Surivam1 pulled ahead of us both, slammed into the condensation unit, and voilà! there was a jewel in his GIC's hand.

"Surivam1, Winner!" the cybervoice echoed in our heads, as the strobe lights flashed on and off to celebrate the moment. But before I could pull my headset off, Dubdub2's GIC disappeared abruptly like a flame that had just blown out, leaving me and Surivam1 looking at each other. I floated slowly in the simulated zero G, not comprehending right away.

But as we were soon informed, Dubdub2 had died. In Analog. It was Station Riskfind's protocol that all gamers had to stay on Riskfind while playing and not access the game remotely. This was a security measure and meant to limit cheating. I think it also kicked a little extra income their way through overnight stays and food. So I was in my private room on Riskfind when I pulled off my headset in alarm and the beautiful visuals in my sight faded to dark.

Oh, I forgot to tell you, I'm blind.

Allow me to introduce myself. I'm Sofia Goodrek, Private Eye. Though basically human-shaped, I'm considered a mutant due to my lack of eyes. Yeah, so my cells mutated at the beginning of me. I can't deny that. And I don't even have any sort of opening for orbitals like most people do, just skin. And sometimes, instead of treating me like your friendly neighborhood mutant, people act like I'm a monster. As if this is something to be whispered about, to be ashamed of in our shiny perfect world.

But I don't want to whisper it at all. I want to shout it out loud. Even though in space there's no sound, the sentiment is the same.

Everyone else I meet is perfect. They have to be, since they started in 1.5 mL Eppendorf tubes in special hatcheries. My cells were nurtured there too, but my genetic engineer fell asleep or was flirting or something when the mutation started growing. In any case, he didn't catch it in time. On Old Earth a few centuries ago, a good percentage of Earthers were blind just from toxins, wear and tear, and mutations like mine. Five hundred years later, that number went to 0.

Then, against all odds, I happened. Welcome to the lottery.

I do have some tools, like my little hand-held scanner. I carry it in my palm. It's flat and fitted with sensors. My scanner absorbs images that then stimulate the nerves in my hand, which allow neurological patterns to replicate images in black and white in my brain.

It's really a sheer stroke of luck that I've made it this far, growing up to be a 25-year-old female private eye living on a space station outside of Alpha Centauri, since it's centuries after the Old Earth burned out. I think my genetic engineer's feelings of guilt, plus my parents' interest in adopting an unusual child, kept me alive. My adoptive parents were sweet, but they died when I was young. And although I couldn't be fitted with anything prosthetic – no eye nerves – the scanner is sufficient. So it's not all bad.

I thought back to when I'd met Dubdub2. As required by gaming protocol, that morning all four of us had assembled our characters on the front deck prior to the competition, and I got to meet my competitors in cyberspace.

She was a famous scientist, or so they said. She had a sparkly voice and didn't try to shake my hand. With my specially adjusted headset, the visuals made her look totally old school, with thick-framed glasses and a lab coat. I was struck by the glasses, as no one wears those anymore. On her, they were purely a statement. While I was admiring them, she turned to me and said, "After the game, let me give you my card so you can contact me when you want to do something about those eyes." I didn't think she could do much, but I was touched by her kindness.

Surivam1, whose character was all in red with a blob of black hair pointing up from his head, seemed to snarl at me. He said, "Mutants don't belong in games. So watch yourself. Oh, sorry, you can't!"

"Don't be so sure!" I countered. He snorted.

As Dubdub2's death sank in, I sent a pocketpod message to my contact, Card, and he gave me the go-ahead to investigate since Riskfind had already contacted him for help.

He asked me if I had my weapon, the neural interruptor. It delivers a laser-like beam to the subject and temporarily interrupts neurological functions. Usually they fall into a seizure-type state. It doesn't last long, and they recover, but while they're immobilized they can be arrested.

I messaged him back, "Yes, always."

Having gotten the go-ahead and removed my gaming gear, I made my way to the main deck using my scanner. I found Riskfind's manager surrounded by staff, but when he saw me he took me into the mazes underneath the ship to talk.

The station didn't need a captain, since it has no need to navigate. It has a series of 200-pound gyroscopes on its bottom deck. They turn 6,000 times per minute to keep it stable and hold it at the right altitude. The ship isn't going anywhere, so they just need a manager, someone to order supplies, make sure the gaming equipment is maintained, and other similar tasks.

The gyroscopes kept a low vibration going in the room next door, but we were in a small chamber that looked like a storage unit to me, and there was nowhere to sit.

"Too many people up above," he said. He was a slow talker with a low resonant voice and a faint odor of clean space station smell, all carbon chains and lemon. My scanner showed him to be a tall, somewhat bent-over man with droopy eyes. His voice somehow cut through the low rattling and rumbling that reverberated in my ears, although he had to yell a bit.

"We can talk here!" he shouted. "No one can hear us now. Are you familiar with the game of Throwback?"

"Yes," I responded. "I use a specialized headset to be able to play, remember? Your crew set it up for me."

"You?" he questioned. "But you're—"

"Yes," I affirmed. "I'm blind."

There was a pause while he tried to digest the idea of blind people playing games.

"Yes—well." He patted his desk, the soft palms resonating on the metal exterior. This seemed to comfort him. "Right," he said.

"Can you tell me the identity of the gamer Dubdub2?"

"That I can," he said. "Everyone knows her. Carina Rock. She's famous, a genius scientist."

"Can you take me to examine her body?"

"What? No, she's not here."

"What do you mean? She has to be here. That violates Riskfind's gaming law."

The manager shuffled his feet and cleared his throat again. "Well, for her and her company we made an exception. She's a famous scientist, makes a lot of money, and she couldn't leave her home location easily. So we made an accommodation for her," he said, and then added, "And they paid us quite well."

"What kind of accommodation?" I asked.

"She would stay at her office when she gamed," he said. "And we got her hooked up when we found out she was a fan of Throwback, the fun space station game."

He was a manager, not a captain, and always looking to showcase his wares.

He continued, "She was able to sign onto the game when she was on break at work. She was the only exception."

"Where is her office?"

"At WeRGen, on their commercial liner," he said. "I could call them for you."

"That's very kind, but I'll find it," I said and fled the store-room, heading for fresh air up above.

IT WASN'T HARD to find out where the WeRGen station was located, and it wasn't too far away, just a few hours by shuttle. The ship was called the *Hummingbird*.

Aiming my handheld scanner through the observation

window, I "saw" the sleek lines of the *Hummingbird* as we pulled up next to it to dock. However, when I disembarked and stepped onto its main deck, what I noticed was the soft plushness of the carpeting and how faint the sounds were from the engines.

Even though notified ahead of time, the CEO didn't have time to meet with me, so another staff member was coming to speak with me about what had happened.

I waited in an atrium of sorts. I heard brisk footsteps approaching, high-heeled shoes on a hard floor. So I inferred that this staff member was probably a woman.

"My name is Aziza," she said upon entering the room. "You can call me Azi for short." Her voice was crisp and even.

My scanner showed her hand approaching abruptly in my direction. The speed of her movement was startling. And she had quite the grip, almost vise-like. After she released my hand, I shook mine to get the blood flowing.

There had been something almost rote in the handshake. I couldn't quite place it.

"We are so glad you are here, Ms. Goodrek," Azi said. "Do you need help? It must be awful not to be able to see."

My handheld scanner showed she was wearing a nice suit, all drapes and folds, and her voice reflected self-assurance. I felt a little underdressed in my utilitarian jumpsuit.

"No thanks, I'm fine," I assured her. "It's important that I view the body as soon as possible. Can you take me to the location where she died?"

"We have water and snacks," Azi offered.

I waved off the snacks but registered that a commercial space station must be a cut above the norm, with more money to spare and snacks to offer.

Azi walked me back into the mazes of the ship, toward Dubdub2's laboratory. We passed groups of people involved in technical discussions in hushed tones.

"We're always involved in research," Azi said, "it doesn't matter what the hour."

She continued, "Her real name was Carina Rock, and she was one of our star-earning scientists here at WeRGen. Whatever she touched turned to rhodium. I'm assuming you've heard of her?"

"Not until right before the game," I said. "I only knew her as Dubdub2."

"Have you heard of Megafood?"

"Yes, I have," I said.

"She invented and perfected that whole concept of instant food production offered through a miniature crystalline printer that creates foodstuffs from various bases. I really have to say it made us a lot of money."

I followed her through a doorway into the labs. "Here's where she was murdered," Azi said.

"What makes you think she was murdered?" I asked.

The word sounded obscene. Just like blindness, murder

was not a thing that could happen in our new and improved society, after our narrow escape from old burned-out Earth.

"I find it odd that you would ask that, given you found her before we did!" she pointed out.

"I witnessed her GIC being destroyed," I said. "I didn't see her die in real life."

Azi laughed briefly and said, "Do any of us know what's real?" She continued, "We found her on the floor. There are marks on her neck. We think she was strangled."

She turned abruptly to walk over to a wall system. From the scanner, I could see there were furniture and things in disarray, items on the floor, the chair knocked over. There had been a struggle.

I knelt in the area where her body had fallen, using the scanner to take DNA samples. These I pressed into a synthetic fixative and scanned to Card from my pocketpod. He'd examine the samples as soon as he could.

"How long was she gone before she was found?" I asked.

"Under an hour," Azi answered. "She was pretty busy and went to a lot of meetings. So it looks like she was gaming between her appointments. To unwind, you know. Our company culture encourages that kind of thing."

"Isn't there a headset?" I said, inspecting the counter tops. "This is an old-school game requiring a headset."

"I don't know what she used," Azi said. "I don't do that."

"Was anything removed from here?" I asked. "It's a crime

scene, isn't it? She died here." Standing back up, I asked, "What was her current research, do you know?"

"Normally it would be proprietary information that we wouldn't give out, but, given the circumstances, I can make an exception for you. She had been putting the final perfecting touches to her new code, the Conversion Code. We own the rights, of course, so she left us quite a legacy."

Even now, with the burnt Earth behind us, money still held sway.

"Do you think this is why she was murdered, for this Conversion Code?" I asked.

"We don't know. She basically worked alone. The code she developed was a fail-safe that could be introduced into any system, robotic or organic, and correct any anomalies. It was the virus of all viruses. It could deconstruct and neutralize anything that didn't belong or make sense. She made it so none of us here at WeRGen would ever have to work again."

"Of course we'll keep working," she added generously, "to continue to benefit spacekind." It sounded like she didn't want me to think her totally selfish. It didn't really work.

"She sounds like a genius," I agreed. "And who wouldn't want this amazing code?"

"Yes, we had to keep it locked up and guarded."

"So there weren't any others who were aware of this?"

"A few," she said. "I could provide you with their names, but they are all accounted for."

"In what way?" I asked.

"Everyone who knew about the Conversion Code, the few who knew, were all at a conference on another research station that day. We checked their communications and all their alibis check out. We've already run the DNA. There is no clear way to establish guilt."

"I'll be running my own as well," I said. "What were your results?"

"Inconclusive, incomplete, partial," she listed.

We'll see, I thought. "Can I please see the body?" I asked.

"Oh!" she responded. "How do you mean?"

"I have my scanner here," I assured her. "And other tools that can assist."

"Oh!" her voice seemed strained. "Is that legal? It sounds like something *we* should have invented."

"Nope, it isn't," I tossed back airily. "Being blind isn't strictly legal either, so nothing else that goes with it is legit."

We walked in silence a bit further down another passageway.

"Would there be any other reason for someone to be jealous of her? Besides the Conversion Code?" I asked.

"I couldn't say," she said somewhat dismissively. Then, "Here's the body."

Carina's body was kept in a lab that was doubling right now as a morgue, with temps turned down to a cold 2 centigrade. I carefully examined her skin, including her face and hands, for signs of fending off or other injuries. The neck did indeed have bruises, but not what you would expect. These were thin marks, not made by hands. With her headset on she would have been an easy target for her attacker. This would have been a silent attack from behind, I guessed. I finished examining her neck, and, moving upwards, found some marks on her ears.

"There're marks on her outer ears," I said. "Looks like some lacerations on the outsides, and also the forehead."

"She was strangled, Ms. Goodrek," the young woman insisted.

It looked like something had been pressed into her head and neck. "Where is the headset?" I asked.

She didn't answer.

"Or can you direct me to someone who can answer my questions?" I asked. I quickly took some samples from under Carina's fingernails, sending those to Card as well.

"There was no headset at the scene," she insisted again. She turned abruptly.

Do I need to conduct a Turing test here? I thought. Azi's answers were repetitive and frankly didn't sound human. She's got to be an android, I concluded.

It was a little unusual but not completely so. Some companies found androids preferable to humans in assistant roles.

Her skin was probably high-level polychloroprene, which wouldn't degrade like other materials, and felt fleshlike. Her movements were likely powered by a sophisticated capacitor that handled all her reactions and expressions. She gave me *sonzaikan*, the sense of being in the presence of a human, but she couldn't maintain the façade for long.

I had taxed her *sonzaikan*osity.

"Thank you," I said. "I'll return to my quarters now, to go over the material."

"Understood," she said. "I'll guide you there."

WeRGen had assigned me some very nice quarters to work from and sleep in if I wanted to. Back at my room, I was at a loss. DNA inconclusive, and all the possible suspects, all who had worked with Carina on the Conversion Code, had been at a conference together on that same day. We could check through their communications that day, but quite frankly it would be impossible for one of them to have left the conference, made the trip to kill someone, and then returned to the conference, all in just an hour on lunch break.

She had been killed during the game. The gamers were the only other people who might know where she was at the time of her death. Everyone else at the commercial station had been gone and had airlock-tight alibis. They'd been accounted for at the conference.

I called up a list of the gamers for that day. Besides myself and Dubdub2, there were CTpax and Surivam1.

Technically I had the power to detain them all, but practically I had no idea who they were or might be. Their locations could be extracted from their character identity profiles, but I would need some assistance.

Turning to my wall panel, I voice-activated it and called on Flick, my coder friend. She and I had spent a good deal of our childhoods together in our livables, me a blind orphan and she an angry incorrigible. She currently lived on a station near a black hole, a great place for someone with her urge to roam.

She answered. My scanner showed her hair parted and braided in knots, supporting something like an old-style gravity-determined playground with little slides and a swing.

"Zat, Soph!" she greeted me.

"Hey Flick!"

"In need indeed?" she queried. Flick and her fellow stationettes spoke a black-hole slang all their own. Being on the edge of annihilation justified a creative take on words.

"Yes, I need some IDs of gaming characters. An old-school headset game. Throwback."

"You play Throwback?" she said. "Retro!"

"If I give you their game IDs, will that be enough?"

"Names nuff," she said.

I provided Flick with their game names and the location, date, and time of the game.

"Contact me with the info," I said. "Love the hair."

"Gravity pulls!" she said. We clicked off.

I checked the results of the DNA that WeRGen had taken, inconclusive results showing human DNA mixed with some inorganic materials.

But a different thought struck me. The lack of *sonzaikan*. The inhumanly strong gripping handshake. Inorganic DNA. The missing headset. Should I feel nervous? As a machine, Azi could be very strong. If I had to take her on, could I deactivate her somehow?

And if she had killed Carina, someone had programmed her to do so.

Right then my pocket pod vibrated. I usually liked it to ring, but when I was on a case I liked everything stealthy and silent. I never knew who might be listening.

I scanned it so I could read the contents of the message. It was from Flick. I activated the wall panel.

"Found 'em!" she said triumphantly.

"Nice!" I said with gratitude. "Who are they?"

"First there's CTpax, name of Simon Ngozi, speculator, from Station Particle Q. Rich, loaded, and a gamer's gamer. Goes all the time. He drops a lot of rhodium when he's there. I don't think he's your guy, the murderer."

"Probably not," I said. "Too much to lose. But I can check him out anyway."

"Second, Surivam1. Research scientist, lives on science station Wasserburg. His real name is Evers Noone. He's a new gamer."

"He's never been to Riskfind before?" I asked.

"No, but here's the kicker, he used to work directly with

Carina. Research assistant. He left WeRGen without notice, just took off."

"Azi never mentioned him," I said. "He's got the strongest connection to her. That's who I'll start with, then. Could be something."

Flick nodded, swings swinging. "Check in if you need something else," she said, and the screen went blank.

In order to successfully have access to Carina, the suspects would have to live or work within 400,000 km of the *Hummingbird*. Otherwise, space wind and radiation could make the distances hard to cover.

I hailed Evers from my panel. I had my badge up by my face so he would get the idea.

"Yeah what?" he said unpleasantly. "Oh it's the blind freak of nature calling! What is it, I'm busy."

"And this is you on a good day?" I retorted. "Congrats on your win. I'm calling you on official business."

"Get on with it," he said.

"I'd like to know where you were in Analog, two days ago when Carina was killed."

"Carina! Who's that?" he said sarcastically.

"Your previous lab director," I said. "Your ex-boss and colleague."

"Why are you asking?"

"I'm a private eye, and you're a murder suspect, due to your prior relationship with Carina."

He laughed without pleasure. "I'm being interrogated by this … this … abnormality? An eyeless private eye."

"Mutancy is a norm in nature—" I started to retort.

"Nature! Who cares about nature! You want to know where I was in Analog when Carina was killed? Right here! Right here in my lab!"

His lab was inside the 400,000-km circle I had identified.

"Why weren't you on the Riskfind?" I asked. "Gaming protocol."

"They made accommodations for me, as a past employee of WeRGen. They liked the money. I just gamed from my lab."

Riskfind's manager had lied to me. Carina wasn't the only one who had paid under the table to game off ship.

"I need to talk with you," I said.

"What about?"

"Her death," I said. "And how you might be involved."

He suddenly became very intent and his voice level. "I didn't kill her, but she deserved to die," he said. "You know why? Or haven't you bumbled blindly into it yet?"

I waited.

"She didn't invent the Conversion Code," he said. "She stole it. You can't steal ideas and expect nothing to happen."

"Can you prove what you just said?" I asked.

He turned off the connection in response.

It was getting late, but my pocket pod rang. It was from Card. DNA results.

There was no human DNA except the victim's. But under the fingernails, polychloroprene cells. The hairs rose on my neck. What if the android was monitoring my communications?

I needed to get off this ship. Now.

I quickly gathered some things. I left the equipment on so that they—whoever—would think I had just stepped out.

I stepped into the passageway and stopped dead. The power had suddenly gone out. That meant not only communications would be down, but the air circulation, and of course the lights. Androids didn't need air, and androids could navigate in the dark.

I quickly made my way, light-footed, down the passageway. I wanted to make one more visit to Carina's lab to grab her computer system.

And then I heard it. The soft footstep of someone, or some *thing*, wearing high heels and hoping not to be noticed. Slow, measured, stalking, toes only, with a soft reflex slap as the remainder of the shoe flapped up against her heel.

Well, she might have *sonzaikan*, but not enough. A real woman would have taken off the damn heels.

Moving quickly and softly, I kept my hand lightly on the wall, using the scanner only to avoid tripping. There were faint fingernail-sized lights running along the length of the passageway, operating on batteries no doubt.

As I went into Carina's lab, I took the module and tucked

it into my flight suit. I could hear the footsteps, and now they were hurried and not caring if they made sound. She must be very sure of herself.

I decided to hide in a utility closet next to the door. As I pulled the door closed, my feet tangled in some cords. Reaching down, I realized it was a headset. Really? She'd hidden it in the closet?

I tried to make a little space for myself. I could feel there were hanging jumpsuits, and the tiny lights along the carpeting shone under the door. It was enough for me to identify other objects. My scanner showed some old electrical equipment, cans of paint, some bucket-type things.

I held my breath as the footsteps stopped outside the lab. I had to school myself to breathe slowly so I didn't hyperventilate. The image of what had happened to Carina was there in front of me. This android was the monster, not me. I didn't know if I had the strength to fight her off. She was polychloroprene with a series of actuators throughout her structure. If I could damage just one of them, it could disable her. Meanwhile I was hoping the other scientists were working on getting power restored. I was aware that Azi was very strong. She had ripped Carina's headgear off and perhaps strangled her with it.

I was straining to hear but didn't know why there was nothing, no sound. I was hoping she would leave and then I could make my way to the ground floor to the shuttle bay.

In self-defense, I crouched. If she opened the door to my closet I would have to act immediately.

A quick thought flitted through my mind. What if Azi hadn't done anything and I damaged an android for no reason? And yet, there had been polychloroprene under Carina's fingernails. I armed myself with a can of paint. The neural interrupter would do nothing.

The door opened suddenly and I launched myself low and forward, taking out her legs and knocking her down. I thought that would disable her computer's thinking for a moment, but it didn't.

She immediately reached up to choke me, her strong hands reaching around my throat. This was obviously a thing with her.

And this was not a fending-off move, this was not to push me away. She was pulling me in to kill me.

I threw the paint at her face. She might be able to see in the dark, but with her eyes completely painted shut she wouldn't be able to see anything at all.

She gave a scream that was part human and part metallic protest. She released her hands from me to clear her vision.

I feel ya, sister, I thought. You haven't had a few decades of practice with that situation.

Crouching by her, I took the headgear and wrapped the cords around her legs, tying a quick knot. She was still a fighter, grabbing at my hair to immobilize me and trying to pull me into her stranglehold again.

But as she sat up to fumble with the headset and free her legs, I searched with my thumb for an actuator in her neck. An android like her would be filled with these little motors, and crushing one could mess with the whole system.

Feeling along her neck and pressing in several places, I finally found one of the hard button-shaped actuators through her skin covering. There was a scary moment of scrambling as I used both hands to crush through the skin, and she was trying to get up but kept falling. I guess "untie my feet" wasn't in her software package. But I finally pushed with all my might and she flopped back down, still. I'm not sure how much time I had before her internal computer diagnosed the problem and got her up and going again.

As I stood up, adrenaline raging, the power went back on. I felt air flow, the hum of computers, and my scanner lit up my arm so I could "see" the light. I felt relief. Certainly I could get out of here now.

But as I headed to the exit, I heard approaching footsteps, and Evers Noone stood at the door. My scanner showed all the lights were on and he stood outlined in the doorway, a nice target. But apparently he didn't know I had the neural interrupter in my pocket.

"You trashed my android," he said, aggrieved.

"*Your* android? She tried to kill me!" I said. "And I need to take her in for killing Carina. We need to analyze her programming."

"You're smarter than I thought," he said.

"And I thought you were in your lab," I said.

"Pretty simple to fake a location," he said. "I was here on the *Hummingbird* the whole time. Simple code to change coordinates."

"Did you program Azi to kill?" I asked. That would explain how he could get to Carina without actually being in the lab with her.

"Have you heard of the Conversion Code?" he asked me. "I made it. I worked on it for years. And she stole it. She took credit for it. It's the greatest invention of my life, and she stole it without a thought. Where does that leave me?" he asked. "Where does it leave me?"

I stayed silent.

"I'll tell you where. Nowhere! Now I'm a humdrum research assistant working on junk, when I could have made all the money and been famous. She betrayed me!"

Now we were getting to it. "That's horrible," I said, to encourage him.

He laughed. "Horrible? She destroyed me!" he said. "Now I have to reinvent myself. But why? Why should I? She's the one who should be destroyed."

"So you programmed Azi to do it? To kill Carina?" I asked.

"Program?" he sneered. "Babies program. I created a masterpiece. I gave Azi a special virus, and the virus's sole function was to keep Azi from killing Carina. Then I introduced the Conversion Code, which reversed that function, since it was an identified virus. Reversing the function logically prompted Azi to kill Carina. I did the same with you. I thought you'd be easy."

"Surprise surprise," I said.

"Well, you've got to go," he said. He said it like he was saying, "We have to dispose of the trash." Evers Noone was the real monster, I reflected. Not me or even Azi.

"What if we clear your name?" I asked, reaching into my pocket. That's right, I was that bold. I'm pretty sure he didn't think that a blind mutant would carry a weapon. And why would he?

"Could you do that, clear my name?" he asked, almost wistfully.

I shot him through my pocket. The neural interrupter caused a seizure-like episode, temporarily immobilizing him. He fell like a stone.

Using my scanner to avoid his body on the way to the doorway, I was relieved to hear the commotion of several pairs of footsteps running in my direction.

"Down here!" I heard someone yell.

"Ms. Goodrek, what happened to you? Is that paint?"

I imagine I was a sight, although I couldn't confirm this, but I had almost been strangled, I was covered in paint of a color I didn't know, and had other scrapes and bruises, not to mention my hair. I think my jumpsuit had a rip on the shoulder.

Another staff member said, "Call the medic."

I spoke loudly and authoritatively. "Evers Noone and Aziza are under arrest for the murder of Carina Rock. They will be transported shortly to a holding facility."

There was a collective gasp. Then, "We'll take care of them. Security!"

Where had security been all this time, by the way? Probably trying to locate the cause of the power outage. An old distraction ruse.

As the medics arrived, trying to persuade me to get onto a stretcher, I said, "About the Conversion Code..."

"Yes?" somebody said.

"Deactivate it," I said. "Make it illegal. Keep it under lock and key."

There was a hesitation. It would mean a huge loss of revenue, but I had a feeling the scientists at WeRGen would come up with another lucrative idea.

"We'll look into it, Ms. Goodrek," came the answer.

And that's how a mutant saved the universe from a code capable of converting anything to something destructive. All in a day's work for me, Sofia Goodrek, Private Eye.

The Fate of Sunlight
by Luka Dowell

BLOOD-ORANGE SUNLIGHT SPILLED across the tiled floor and cast a stretched shadow of the barred prison window. It pooled around the drain in the corner of my cell. I tried to envision the metal rim encrusted in gems but all I could imagine was my own blood, dripping. I wanted to pretend the creaky cot was my throne in a kingdom of fire. What does a god have to fear about death?

"So what are *you* in for?" The voice, clear but delicate, brought me out of my fantasy and the pool on the floor became water again. I turned to the partition between my cell and the next, metal bars, just like the window. There was a woman there, poised in the shadow just out of the sunlight's reach, but her face was illuminated enough. Her coiled black hair glowed like embers, warming her dark skin. Her eyes were soft but bright enough to betray her curiosity, and something about them was familiar. She was certainly younger than me, and by no small margin. She looked innocent enough, but she held herself as though she felt something in the air I couldn't.

"Was it murder?" she asked, with a bold grin.

"Nothing like that," I responded, flatly. She wasn't satisfied.

"Theft? Arson?" she pressed on, evidently excited to talk to someone. I wondered how long she'd managed to evade my notice, waiting for some sort of interaction. I decided to indulge her; I had no reason to hide anything at this point.

"I stowed away," I replied. Her face lit up like a child's would.

"How romantic," she said. "He stows away on a spaceship to start a new life on a faraway planet." After a pause, she added, "Am I right?"

"Demeter," I said. She gave me a look as though she'd known all along.

"You're a farmer, then." Her voice was less enthusiastic.

"Sorry I'm not more interesting," I offered. I gestured to the meager prison cell around me. "Sometimes plans don't work out how we want them to."

"So true," she responded. I wondered what stories someone her age had to tell. At the very least, I wanted to know what a young girl could have done to get locked up. "But wait, they'd put you in a prison like this for stowing away?"

I simply shrugged.

"Right, it's a bit more complicated than that, isn't it?"

"You could say that," I said and left my cot to meet her closer to the partition. My shadow passed ominously over the patch of sunset on the floor. "Either way, I'm a dead man." I had until the sun set, and then I'd be taken to my execution. I assumed she was in the same boat.

"You don't need to remind me," she replied. Her expression lost its energy as she confirmed my suspicion. Her watchful eyes dropped to the floor, where the little patch of fire had made its way further across the tiles. She studied it for a moment, probably seeing something far more engaging than a few last rays of sunlight.

She raised a single pointer finger up in the air, drawing a shadow across the floor. She wiggled it around enthusiastically before adding a second.

"What are you doing?"

"Shadow puppets," she replied. "Did you ever make shadow puppets as a kid?"

"No," I said, and she frowned at me.

"That's too bad," she said. "They're a good way to pass the time when you're on the verge of death." She twisted the fingers on her right hand into a shape that cast the crude shadow of a face onto the wall. "Can you guess what this one is?"

"I have no idea," I said. I had no interest either, but I didn't want to let her down. She was doing what little she could to be happy, and I only wished I could do the same.

"It's a rabbit," she said. "An innocent rabbit, happy as can be." For emphasis, she bounced her hand up and down a few times. "Now guess what this one is," she said in a lower voice. She held three fingers up: two fully extended, and one bent halfway.

"Some trees?" I suggested. She looked disappointed with my answer.

"It's a family," she said. "Mom, Dad, and the baby. They're very happy together." *I miss my family,* I thought to myself. *I'll never get to say goodbye.*

"Good for them," I responded finally, trying to hide my regret.

"Now look," she said, as she lowered one finger, "Dad is gone. He never said where he was going." My heart dropped as low as the puddle on the floor. I felt guilt wash over me like my kingdom of fire, only colder. *There's no way she's doing this on purpose*, I had to remind myself, as her innocent shadow puppets hit way too close to home.

"Good for them," I said again without thinking, immediately wishing I could pull the words back out of the air. *Now you just sound insensitive. She's obviously hurt.*

"No, it's not," she replied.

"No, it's not," I agreed. "I'm sorry." She shook her head dismissively.

"I'm Maya, by the way."

"Nice to meet you, Maya."

"And you are?" Maya looked at me, waiting for my reply.

"No one," I answered. She rolled her eyes at me.

After a moment, she continued, "How much do you know about Earth?"

"Nothing," I lied. "I mean, I know *of* it." *Does she know who I am?* The pointedness of her questions was starting to worry me. It was almost as if she was trying to make me reveal something. I wasn't used to telling my secrets.

"I'm from Earth," said Maya. "I'm a teacher there. Or, I was. I guess it doesn't really matter now."

"People still live there?" I asked, feigning ignorance. Deep down it was an honest question: *Is my family still alive?*

"A few of us. Scavengers, mainly. There isn't much left, but it's home." *Sounds about right.* It was nice to spend time with a fellow Earthling, even if I'd never admit anything to her. "Look, the stars are coming out," she said, pointing out her window.

"I don't see them."

"You're too tall. Bend down a little," said Maya. I bent my knees and looked up through my own window. In the waning sun, pinpricks of starlight were just beginning to appear, dusting the red sky. "The second sun won't rise for a while longer." She stopped and looked directly back at me as she added, "But we won't be around to see it." Maya was right. Our time was nearly up.

I raised one shiny metal hand into the air and passed it through the patch of fiery sunlight hanging over me. My fingers gleamed with orange and red, and it was so beautiful it almost didn't look like blood. I watched my shadow dance across the wall opposite my cell. The joints in my fingers whirred with energy. *How did she make the rabbit again?*

"What happened to your hands?" Maya asked. It had probably been on her mind for a while.

"Farming ... accident," I replied, hoping she would buy it. She probably didn't, but at least she stopped asking. As I watched the sunlight gleaming on every greased joint, I almost felt pain. The sight of frostbitten fingers, cold and dead, was hard to forget. I reached for the warmth of the light streaming through the barred window as if I needed to thaw again. As if the sunlight was there to save me, and not just prolong my demise.

"How did you afford them?" she asked, just when I was hoping to drop the subject entirely.

"I worked it off in time," I said. Another lie. There was no way I could ever really afford them, but I didn't need Maya knowing that.

"I believe you," she responded, in a voice that said she didn't. She was young, but not stupid, a teacher, after all. Still, I didn't want her pressing any further.

At that point, Maya retreated into the shadows, and a creaking whine a moment later confirmed she had returned to her cot. I followed her example, and tried to imagine my throne again, still to no avail. My wishful thinking wasn't helped by the deathly feeling looming over both of us.

After a few minutes, judging by the creeping sunlight on the wall, Maya said, "They're going to send me up in a shuttle and open the airlock."

"Why?"

"It was the warden's idea. He knows I have a fear of dying in space."

"You know the warden?" To that, Maya didn't respond. I realized I might be able to pry more information out of her than I thought, and that she might be far more important than she let on. I decided I would spend my last few minutes trying to find out. "How do you know the warden?" I asked again.

After a long silence, Maya finally responded weakly, "I don't want to die." Silence settled again. And then, even fainter, "I don't want to die."

"We're both going to die. That wasn't my question." She didn't even acknowledge my reply. "There isn't anything we can do now."

There was no point in denying it. *I'm being sent to execution soon too. Am I facing the same fate?*

Maya began to cry, not slowly, but suddenly and powerfully. She had moved to the other side of her cell, where the last dregs of sunlight flickered away. The few remaining rays illuminated the bars that separated her from the darkened hallway, and she was clasping them with both hands as if sunlight was something tangible. Each handful that came back empty only served to worsen the sobbing. "I don't want to die," she repeated, hands now grasped around the prison bars. And then, barely a whisper, "I'm not done here yet." As the last of the light slipped out of her hands, she sank to the ground in silence.

Maya didn't move for at least a whole minute, during which I couldn't even think to get up or move towards her. We sat in silence. Soon I could hear her begin to hyperventilate, and her whole body shivered like an engine waking up.

"Maya?" I called. She didn't respond, or even make any indication that she heard me. Her shadow was ominous and distorted against the wall. "Maya?" I tried again. No response.

Several seconds of heavy silence passed before I watched her rise to her feet, grasping the bars for support. She looked barely capable of maintaining her standing position, wobbling on shaky legs. But then, she held her hands more firmly around the bars, and her breathing slowed down considerably. The tears had stopped. She was a ghost as darkness settled over her face and shoulders.

In an instant, the silence was shattered by an ugly, wild scream. It was enough to jolt my senses into urgent action. I leapt up and reached for the partition separating the two of us. Maya drew her hands back and took several steps away from the bars. "Maya, calm down," I said. Her whole body seemed to be shaking from the very core. A final dash of sunset flared around her, and she glowed like magma.

Then, without warning, Maya bashed herself against the

bars, full-force, knocking the wind out of her and sending her crumpling to the floor. Before I could call out, she stood up again, ramming herself into the bars senselessly before even regaining her balance.

"Maya!" I yelled. My voice echoed down the hallway. *If they didn't hear us before, they hear us now.* But it was too late to worry about that. The wall had gone dark, and we were rapidly losing visibility. We were out of time anyway. "Maya, stop!" I called out. I was stunned as she continued to beat herself against the barred prison door, sometimes with fists, sometimes knees, and sometimes her whole body at once in explosions of panic. She was just trying to get out. It was the only thing left to do. I didn't blame her.

I heard the indistinct jabber of personal comms systems coming to life, soon accompanied by heavy footsteps. *Well, we've done it now.* The guards were coming, and fast. I took a seat on my cot, awaiting the inevitable. In an hour I'd be dead, vacuum freeze-dried. Strangely, my life wasn't flashing before my eyes, nor did I have anything profound to say in my final moments. I just hoped my wife and daughter were alive and well somewhere out there.

Maya couldn't be much older than twenty; she was young for a teacher, certainly. I felt quite a bit of compassion for her, though I had only just met her. Something about her brought it out in me. And still, I wondered what she had done to be locked up here, and to know the warden. *They're probably coming to separate us.* I feared now I would never know Maya's secret.

Two burly prison guards in heavy-looking riot gear materialized from the shadowed hallway. In the fast-approaching darkness, it was hard to make out details and impossible to define facial features, but their silhouettes were as clear and sturdy as boulders. One of them carried a flashlight in his left hand and a keyring in the other. The other held an assault rifle at the ready. Maya appeared to be too terrified to move. I tried, and failed, to stand, realizing I was just as scared.

Maya was on the floor, her arms pulled around her knees in a fetal position, obviously not concerned with the water pooled on the tiles. She wasn't even rocking back and forth anymore, and the only indication she was still alive was her panicked and irregular breathing. Every breath was a fight against the urge to collapse.

How can they do this to her? I found my strength enough to get to my feet. My hands felt heavier than usual, as though something was pulling them down. I looked around for any sort of object that could be used as a weapon, but I knew I'd be gunned down in a second for trying.

The guard with the keyring selected a small, polished key and inserted it into the lock on my cell. The armed guard stood by, holding his weapon firmly, but thankfully not pointing it at me. The lock opened with a soft click. After a second of silence, the cell door came crashing open by means of a well-placed kick. They quickly seized me, forcing me face-first against the wall. The concrete was like ice against my cheek. Memories came flooding back and my hands twitched involuntarily in response, ghosting, out of control like the rest of my body. *I can't go back there. Not now.* It burned.

The tears froze as they rolled down my face, raw from exposure. Everything was screaming, my legs, my arms, my pounding heart struggling to keep them alive. Maybe I was screaming too; I couldn't tell. I looked up to meet the icy gaze of the towering man before me. "You won't be completing your contract on me," he said. His hot breath made clouds in the air between us. His grip around my wrists tightened as he plunged my hands further into the liquid so cold I swore I was on fire. He laughed. It was a roaring laugh that dug into my brain. Still he held my wrists, and still I couldn't move. I squeezed my eyes shut and succumbed to the pain.

Soon I realized I couldn't feel my hands at all. My stomach turned as I dared to look. They were blackened and scabbed as though they had been charred, but I knew they weren't burned. It was severe frostbite. I would never use those hands again.

One of the guards must have noticed my hands, because he grabbed them and pulled until I was bent over, my arms behind my back. "You won't be needing these," he said. I struggled, but he was much stronger than I.

"Those aren't meant to come off!" I cried. I heard the click of mechanics detaching, and felt pain shoot down my forearms as wires snapped. I pulled back, but it was too late. My motion only further dislodged the metal from my arms. I felt it deep beneath my skin, like a knife dragging against my shivering muscles. I looked toward Maya. She still wasn't moving, but she was watching, in silence. Her face mirrored the horror I felt. I felt my blood dripping. It splashed swirls of red into the puddle on the floor.

Grasping me by the shoulders with gloved fingers, one of the guards spun me around violently until I was facing the door. "Walk," he commanded. I did. There was nothing I could do to stop him. *Unless ...*

As we crossed the threshold of the doorway, I shifted all of my weight to one side in a last-ditch effort, putting the guard out of position for just a moment, just enough to slam him against the bars. One of them collided straight with his square jaw. He dropped his iron grip on me and I slipped out from behind him.

I stumbled down the damp, darkened hallway, continuing towards what I believed to be an outdoor balcony. *Maybe I can jump off.* Even if I died, it would be a better death than what I faced otherwise.

A scream broke the silence and it stopped me instantly. I tried to remind myself I had no loyalty to Maya. Still, something about that scream made me want to run back and help her, even if I knew I couldn't do anything.

Too late now, I told myself. I didn't have time to stop. If I was lucky, at least one of us could make it out alive. *She means nothing to me,* I thought. *Nothing to me,* I repeated. I got the sense that I was lying to myself. Maybe there was just a certain companionship in sharing a jail cell.

Suddenly, there was something hard and narrow pressed against my neck. I had felt the sensation enough times in the past to know it was a gun barrel. "Walk," the voice from earlier commanded me. "The other way," he added. "There's no exit that way." The other guard chuckled. Hopeless, I turned around and trudged back the way I'd come. We passed my cell, and Maya was gone.

We reached the end of the hallway. Our exit was blocked by a solid steel door with a small window. From my height I could just make out some kind of outdoor complex in the dim twilight. The sky was growing cloudy, and it covered the cracked concrete in shadow.

The guard in front of me shoved the door open with considerable effort and I was hit with a blast of icy air. They guided me into the yard, a struggle for them as every step took significant effort. Without my hands I felt defenseless.

Maya stood in the center of the yard, handcuffed, also held in place by two muscular guards. She wasn't still, rattling the handcuffs violently and screaming, but she was no match for their strength. One of the guards slapped her against the face and she stopped screaming. I felt a pang in my heart, hearing the impact of the blow. I lurched forward, trying to reach her, but I was pulled back painfully by the collar of my shirt.

Before I had time to retaliate, I was on the ground, pinned down across my back and weakened arms. My head hit the ground forcefully, sending sparks flying through my vision. With my hands missing, I was in no position to get up. The concrete was cold.

With my head turned to the side, I could see a small shuttle stationed in the courtyard, barely large enough for one person. The metal was aged with rust and some of the paneling was missing. The door was open, and it was dark inside. I figured it was Maya's shuttle.

By now a substantial crowd of prisoners had gathered around us, all standing in silence. I got the impression Maya was important to them. I wondered again what she had done to get here, especially since she mentioned being from my home planet.

One of the prisoners, a young girl, stood out from the rest of the crowd. Unlike the others, she stood a couple feet in front of Maya. They held eye contact with each other. I didn't hear any conversation; I wondered if they were having some sort of unspoken communication. Eventually Maya turned her head down toward the ground, and I could hear sobbing. The guards dragged the young girl away from her, without a fight.

I noticed a tall woman standing with the guards, in the

same black garb but without any weapons. She stood with a firm posture, her hands together at her waist formally. When she saw Maya, the smirk on her face was unmistakable. I guessed this was the warden.

Maya's struggling became more violent, and soon she was screaming and flailing her arms against her restraints. I found myself silently cheering her on. I didn't struggle, myself. I just watched.

Maya's vicious thrashings eventually overcame her guards' grip, and she leapt away, towards the young girl. For a moment, she was free. I felt the weight on my back shift slightly, and I realized her opportunity was mine.

With all the strength I could draw from my core, I rolled over onto my back, shoving the guard, who was on top of me, to the side. I sat up to push myself to my feet. But when my exposed forearms hit concrete, I remembered the extent of my situation, and before I could attempt another method to right myself, they grabbed me again. I watched helplessly as Maya ran, and there was nothing I could do to stop her when she tripped and fell flat on her face. The guards were back on her in an instant.

When I found Theresa, she was seated cross-legged in the tall grass, crying. The black curls of her hair almost hid the tears streaming down her cheeks. She had a nasty skinned knee peeking out from the hem of her tattered dress. I knelt down beside her and held out a supporting hand. She didn't take it.

Theresa sat on the kitchen table—a wooden plank over several cinder blocks—as I dabbed at her injuries with a wet rag. She said the neighbors' dog had chased her and she'd gotten scared. I didn't ever want to see my daughter scared again.

They forced me in first. I was too cold and tired to put up anything resembling a fight. I was tossed roughly against something large and soft, probably a chair. They threw Maya in next, with even less grace. Her breathing was labored.

"Let this be a lesson to the both of you," the warden shouted. I saw Maya fumble with a thin silver pendant chain around her neck. "A lesson that crime doesn't p—" I didn't get to hear the end of the sentence before the door closed, leaving the two of us defeated and disoriented in complete darkness. We sat in silence, with no sound or motion giving us any idea of what was going on outside.

A tiny electronic beeping noise, like a digital watch, started up suddenly. A moment later, the room was bathed in a faint glow, dim enough that I wasn't sure if I was imagining it or not, until Maya pointed it out. "What's that?" she asked. I realized she was pointing to my shirt. The fiery light was coming from underneath the thin fabric. Suddenly I was aware again of the cold metal ring against my chest. My heart began pounding as I sat motionless, stunned and bewildered.

Theresa is in trouble. And then, *There's nothing I can do.*

A brighter glow illuminated Maya's face in the darkness. Her eyes burned like tiny suns in the light. Something was cupped between her hands now, peeking out bright red through cracks between fingers. We looked at each other for a long while, studying each other. Finally she said, voice cracking, "… Dad?"

She grabbed the ring with tiny hands, chubby fingers closing around the brushed red metal. Her eyes were wide with wonder at the object. "If you ever need me," I said, "press that button and I'll come find you." I pulled the pendant around my neck out from behind my shirt to show her. "Look, I have one too." She nodded in understanding. "Be safe, now."

"Where are you going, Daddy?" Theresa asked me, innocent as could be. I didn't answer.

"Theresa?" I said. "I'm so sorry."

"It's a little late for that," she responded, but she didn't sound mad. "I just want to know—" she paused, then, "Just tell me what you did to get here."

"The hands," I replied. "I stole them."

"They were pretty well lodged in there. It must have been quite the farming accident."

"Torture."

"For?"

"Murder attempt. I was a mercenary."

"You left us to kill people?" She cast her ring aside violently and it clattered to the floor next to me. Her face lost its warm glow.

"We needed money," I replied. "Surely you knew that."

"Why didn't you tell me?"

"You were three."

I heard a soft sniffle in the darkness. My heart was aching in every way it could think to. I just wanted to scream and break the door down, but I knew I'd get nowhere. Instead, I let the conversation sputter out like a dying flame.

Soon there was a powerful rumbling that shook the vessel. I still couldn't wrap my mind around my situation. It seemed inconceivable that we were being sent to die. I wondered if this was the death I had earned. *But surely she doesn't deserve it.*

The rumbling increased into a growl that sent the entire room into tremors and made my already pained heart sink even deeper. I knew enough about spacecraft to understand what was going on. I could feel the force of our ascent weighing down on me as we quickly gained altitude. We'd be dead in a couple of minutes.

"It wasn't supposed to go like this, you know," she said feebly. "It wasn't supposed to go like this at all."

"What do you mean?"

"You want to know what I got in trouble for?" She didn't give me a chance to respond before continuing, "I was on the same flight you stowed away on. I was hijacking the ship."

She's the reason I didn't reach my destination.

"Why?" was all I could think to say. I realized I had no idea what kind of person my daughter was now. There was no way I could guess at her motives for anything.

"To stage a prison break, actually." Her laugh was as hollow as I felt inside.

"Here?"

"There was a raid on our town, looking for people like me. Activists, teachers. I changed my name to hide. They took … they took a lot of people."

"Including the girl that was standing with you."

"A student of mine." She heaved a heavy sigh.

My vision was flooded with blood-orange light. It seared its way into my brain and I shielded my eyes until they could adjust. *Sunlight.*

Theresa found a window. We were watching a sunset, and it was glorious. The star spread its fire over the clouds, their plumes concealing the curvature of the planet below, and bold light shone directly into the shuttle. Theresa stood hunched in the corner. Her hair had regained its ember-like glow. Her shadow hung ominously over the wall opposite her.

I was sprawled across a small black bench stationed in the center of the shuttle, my arms hanging awkwardly from the sides. Across from me was a small control panel with symbols I couldn't read, faded from use. It dawned on me that they must come collect the shuttle and freeze-dried bodies again each time. I wondered how many people had died this way.

"There's a window on the other side, too," Theresa said.

"I can't open the shade." I gestured with my arms. She nodded and inched across the shuttle to the other side. With what sounded like considerable effort, the shade on the window slid open. Brilliant white light flooded the room. The second sun was rising, even bolder than the first.

"It's a happy little rabbit," Theresa said. She held up several fingers against the light streaming in from the window. I turned my attention to the other side of the shuttle. It was indeed a rabbit. "It never did anything wrong," she said. "It was just trying to help the other bunnies it cared about." Finally, she added, "We never did anything wrong."

An alarm blared as the preliminary airlock doors opened, and a hissing sound gradually grew in volume and urgency. Our shadows were cast aside in the glare of light from all directions.

The Shepherd
by Heather Dubois

JUDI SAT IN her office sealed off from the rest of her crew, the people and their germs. Her crew knew what they were doing, she was certain of that. This wasn't their first time and it wouldn't be their last. But it might be hers if she screwed up again.

She couldn't help the knot of doubt that twisted her stomach. A month ago C.J. had had a cold, he was coughing and sneezing, and he'd touched her without washing his hands. What should she have done? She'd needed a shower. She'd felt the germs multiplying on her skin. She forced the memory aside. After all, they'd managed to avoid total disaster. And, she added to bolster her own confidence, C.J. wasn't sick today.

She couldn't mess up like that. If she did, she'd be done. Worse, it would prove true the whisperings of Command, that women should not be on such missions, much less in command. Her failure now would set women back a good couple centuries.

She enjoyed her job, most of it anyway. She shuffled the papers on the desk, tapping the organized pile three times before setting it aside. She straightened the few items sitting on her desk, passing the time while she waited.

Who was she kidding? She was putting her things back where they belonged. C.J. always touched them when he was preparing for a show, and always put them back just slightly out of place. She knew he did it on purpose.

An involuntary shiver passed the length of her spine as she thought about him holding the amber paperweight, and she reached for the hand sanitizer. Her crew always gave her a hard time when she pulled it out, but there was no help for it. Not in her mind anyway. She forced the thought of his germs away, letting them multiply in the depths of her mind until she could shower later. It was show time, and she needed to be on top of things today.

C.J. was giving his final speech, though he didn't know it would be his last. He was oblivious. He'd played his part to perfection. He could not have done better, had he known.

She would tell him soon, while his followers drank in the over-oxygenated air and listened to David Bowie during the intermission. By then it would be too late for him to do anything. And finally his ramblings about quelling the growing population would end. If she had to listen to his rantings one more time ... He repeated his message so many times, even when not in the spotlight, that she sometimes thought his brain was just a CD set to repeat.

She glanced down at the pages she had been unconsciously rolling and unrolling. It was a nervous habit she'd developed on her first mission, to help deal with her proximity to others, fiddling with whatever was in her hands. This was the speech he was currently giving, and she was not overly impressed. She wished she could have written it. But he would not let anyone speak for him. He was too proud for that, too meticulous about every detail. Almost every detail. And it was the one thing he had forgotten to check that would be his undoing.

He had never researched his companions. He hadn't realized that they all knew each other. Judi had planned that well. Each of the twelve joined his following in a different city, with different specialties. Each happened to show up just as they were needed. He had taken that for providence, taken it as a sign he was doing the right thing.

His arrogance was why he had been chosen. He researched every fact used in his speeches, every thought sketched out to the minutest detail. But his staff remained in the shadows. *We were not important enough for him to check. We were his followers, we were harmless.* Or at least that's what he believed.

A knock on her door interrupted her thoughts, and she automatically smoothed the papers on her desk. A brief silence was followed by Drew's excited voice.

"Judi, he's beginning to wrap up his speech." He paused, then added tentatively, "We're still a go, right?"

She sighed. If he was doubting her, they all were. Could she do it? Of course she could.

Without answering, she crossed to the door, tapping the control panel three times before entering her code. Pulling it open she smiled at the youngest of her team. For this mission, he wore his thick blond hair long, tied back into a tail that hung to the middle of his back. Hazel eyes sparkled, adding to the illusion of youth caused by the boyish fullness that rounded his cheeks.

Although irreplaceable for his ability to pilot the craft, and wire or rewire all of the components, he had been relegated to her gopher for this part of the mission because of his apparent age. He could barely pass for eighteen this time. But that only made him more valuable to her since no one gave him a second glance.

She nodded as she stepped into the hall and pulled the door closed behind her. "Good. How is the crowd?" Pressing her hand to a hidden panel in the wall, she waited for the almost imperceptible ping of the electronic lock before falling into step with Drew.

"Unbelievable! Haven't heard a whisper since he started. Gotta give him credit, he commands attention."

She heard the smile in Drew's voice. But it was the content that made the corners of her mouth turn up. C.J.'s ability to command and hold people's interest had been what had caught her eye in the first place when he'd been spouting his nonsense on the street corner in Las Vegas.

"Good ... Everyone in place? This is going to have to be quick if we're to pull it off without trouble." She shot Drew a sideways glance but kept her pace.

Drew nodded and cleared his throat. "Pete, Jim, Phil, and Nate have the doors. They will seal them as soon as the entertainment starts. Matt, Tom, Tadd, and Simon are manning the control booth. Jamie and Jon are in place to deal with the security personnel. It's ill-equipped but still a presence. That means C.J. is all yours."

She saw the shadow of the thought cross his face. *Was she ready, could she do it this time? Could she save the mission?* She could, she knew it, but she'd have to prove it. To Drew and the others.

Judi nodded, then reached for the radio and keyed up the mic. "Any problems?"

Silence filled the hallway for a few seconds before chaos ensued, as all attempted to report readiness at the same time. Typical. They thought as one. Why not act as one too?

Drew stopped outside the control booth, pausing with his hand on the door. "The hologram is ready, I've double-checked. It will hold until we are well underway."

Judi lightly punched Drew on the shoulder. She rubbed her fist on her skirt as she looked past him, eyeing the clock. "As soon as the doors are sealed."

Judi strolled backstage to wait for C.J. with a sealed bottle of water. The whiskey was in his private room. She would allow him a last indulgence, only as it benefited her to keep him relaxed and complacent.

She watched as he finished up his speech. His lean frame stood a mere five feet eight inches, but his presence filled the stage, drawing every eye. She could not see his face from here, but she could almost feel his gaze. She'd watched him deliver his talks so many times before. His vibrant blue eyes continually scanned the audience, making it appear as if he directed his message individually to everyone present. It was part of the allure, part of what drew the crowds. That, along with the slight Welsh lilt to his speech, never failed to draw in the women.

He held the final smile as he stepped behind the curtain. "Did you see that?" C.J. demanded as he picked up a towel to wipe away the light sheen of sweat and that falsely caring smile.

"We've been a bit busy, but Drew says you had the house." She pushed the bottle into his hand.

He nodded, cracking the water with a grimace. "I keep telling you whiskey." He coughed, took a long pull on the bottle, then pushed past her. He let the bottle drop into her hands as the air of superiority crept back into his features. He was still partially in his public mode, but the smile that had been charming onstage faded into his usual arrogant smirk.

"And I keep telling you, water first." She struggled to keep her composure as water sloshed out of the open bottle, over the rim that had touched his lips, and cascaded over her hands. "You know where the whiskey is. Have I let you down yet?" She dropped the bottle onto a random table, took out her sanitizer, then scrubbed her hands on her skirt as she followed him. *Have to keep control.*

He muttered something that she didn't attempt to decipher. It would only prove to piss her off, and she wanted to enjoy this. With the after-show niceties concluded, they lapsed into their usual, awkward silence.

He was their boss, or that was what he thought. And even though the team had been together for thirteen months now, C.J. was still an outsider. He always would be, not only because he preferred it, but because of what he was.

The idea of putting men like C.J. in positions of power annoyed her. Having to play the servant to an obvious inferior pushed her acting abilities – and her nerves – to their limits. But when one of their own was in charge, power went to their heads. Each time she had had to betray them, publicly kill them.

Making others think they were dead was easy. However, one time it had backfired, another of her failures. It had been a messy death, and she couldn't bring herself to touch him, so she'd allowed those followers to bury him before she'd collected the body. To this day, they still talked about him.

Judi broke the silence as she opened the door to his private suite. Stepping back, she let him enter. "I have a couple of suggestions for the next speech." The offer would set him off, but everything was in motion now and she no longer cared. His reign was at an end.

He stiffened and she knew he would bite back the anger, at least for the moment. There were others in the halls, and the last thing he would do was snap at her where someone else could hear.

"Judi, you've been with me over a year now …"

"And you may just want to listen for once." She heard the impatience in his voice but still interrupted him. She wanted to catch him off guard while she began the transition from servant to master.

As the door latched behind her, he whirled, his face now inches from hers. The moment had passed, as she knew it would, and his true personality swelled to fill the room. "You don't have the knowledge I do, you haven't studied the issues. The world is at seven billion people now and will be at nine billion by the middle of the century if we don't do anything." He spat the sentences at her, then strode to the bar to pour a drink.

He wouldn't move or speak again until he'd had at least one glass. He never did. That suited Judi just fine. She closed her eyes, using her sleeve to wipe the spit from her face, steeling herself. *Keep it together, keep it together.* That was the best she could do for the moment. She wasn't going to fail.

While his back was turned she pressed on the wall next to the door. It silently slid back, exposing a control panel. She tapped the top of the keypad three times, then punched in a code. She started to relax as the green *All Access* message turned to a red *Restricted*. He would no longer be able to leave the room without her consent. Of course that meant she was stuck in there with him … and his germs.

The panel clicked back into place as his glass rattled against the bar. She strolled over to the couch, settling in for the evening's entertainment, fighting the perceived sensation of something crawling over her skin. She had to keep him occupied until everything was beyond his control. For now she may as well have a bit of fun with him. Make up for having to play his inferior.

He poured himself a second glass and positioned himself on a bar stool to look down on her. He took another sip, then tapped the glass absently against the bar. "For all the time you have worked for me, you don't seem to understand the problem. We need to slow the fecundity of the world's population before it reaches a point where the Earth cannot sustain it." C.J. took another drink and stared hard at Judi.

"I do understand. I have heard all your speeches, your thoughts on mandating birth control for everyone, of legalizing and mandating abortions." Her voice was soft, low, forcing him to keep his hand still, to keep the glass from rattling so he could hear her clearly. "But you are wrong if you think we agree with you."

His laughter filled the room. "If you didn't agree, why would you be here? Why would everyone be queuing up to listen?"

Judi stood and strode over to him. Using his own technique, she moved close and took the glass from his hand. "I never said *they* did not agree. I said *we*, the twelve of us, do not agree. And it is time to put a stop to it." Her face was inches from his. His breath filled her nostrils, but she forced herself to hold her position. *She had to keep his attention. She couldn't fail.*

C.J. leaned back, and panic flashed across his features. He stood, tipping over the stool as he backed toward the door, a rabbit ready to run. Her eyes must have flashed to their natural violet with her own growing excitement. It happened sometimes, although it galled her when she lost control. Her loss of control was why she'd failed last time. She was ready this time. The faint click of the engines engaging could be heard. Well, she could hear it. She knew C.J.'s human ears couldn't pick it up, not over the steady hum of activity from the arena. She widened her stance as the floor began to vibrate.

A single sharp jolt knocked C.J. off balance. He grabbed the back of a chair to keep himself upright. "Earthquake?" His question seemed more hopeful than anything else. Fear leaked from his eyes and streaked his face.

She had him where she wanted him. She could almost see

the confusion jumping from synapse to synapse as he struggled with an understanding of who, or what, she was.

She shook her head at the question. "The rest of the humans will think so, and you may very well wish it was," she answered as she dropped his whiskey back onto the bar and strode to the wall opposite the door. A control panel appeared and she punched in the code. Another panel drew back, and the pair looked out over the earth. The ground shrinking beneath them calmed her and broadened her smile.

"What the … Who … what are you?" He was at the door now, failing to force his usual measure of calm to his actions. He struggled to push it open, his attention torn between his desire to leave and Judi.

Judi's laugh exploded. She finally dropped all pretenses and let some of her disguise fall away. She stood before him, her skin the pale amber of her race. Her eyes blazed an electric violet and her hair fell in coarse silver strands down her back. She retained the human form. After decades of use she had grown accustomed to it. And she would be back to Earth soon, so best not to get too comfortable in her natural form, even if the stature of the humans was limiting.

"It won't open. You may as well have a seat. You have a bit of a trip ahead of you." She settled back on the couch, smoothing out her skirt, and watched him struggle with the door.

He whirled on her. "I don't care what you are. You take us back. Now!"

His hands shook. His usual calm-under-pressure façade had cracked, but she doubted it would ever disappear completely. He would always attempt to be in control, of himself if nothing else. And he was no longer in control of this, even if he wanted to continue to pretend he was.

"No, I don't think so." She kept her calm. The silence from outside their room meant the others must have attended to the rest, calmed the crowds from the "earthquake." Told them they were safe where they were for the moment. It would be another few minutes or so before any of them would begin to suspect.

"There are more of us than there are of you." He took a few tentative steps toward her. Testing the floor or his own inner strength she could not tell, but she did hear the crack in his voice.

"True, but they are penned up in the arena. Not much they can do from there." He wouldn't know, but all of the doors leading out would now be restricted. Humans would not be able to open them. As usual, they would riot eventually. Some would die. They always did. But they kept well.

C.J. took another few steps in her direction. She could see his anger welling, and she stood to meet his challenge. Only now, instead of his looking down on her five-foot-four human frame, she stretched to her full height, looming above him, her hair just missing the twelve-foot-high ceiling.

Her size halted his advance but not his mouth, his voice a

shallow whisper he had to force from his throat. "You can't expect the world not to miss an entire stadium, can you?"

Just like all the others. When they knew force wouldn't work, they would try to reason. "True. Even you humans would miss something like that if it just disappeared. However, since we can predict when your earthquakes will happen, we have arranged our departure to coincide with a fairly large one."

He gaped at her, at a loss for words. It was soothing for once to not hear him speak, to know he had no answer prepared.

"This ship will not be missed, and none of your bodies will either, considering there is a major rent in the Earth's surface where this arena used to stand. We left a few dazed, unconscious survivors, and copies of the rest to be found buried under tons of rubble."

The copies were close enough to fool human technology, but her kind could easily tell the difference, and they preferred the real thing to a manufactured reproduction. She strode casually over to the window. It was a shame the scene was too far away for him to see clearly, but they had a schedule to keep. They were already a year behind because she had failed to seize the last opportunity. "By the time the city is on its feet again, they won't even think to look too closely at the bodies. I suppose when we return, there will be a memorial plaque near the hole that swallowed this stadium."

"You can't do this." He headed for his abandoned glass.

"We already have. It's not the first time, you know." Her gaze locked with his when he turned back around. She could feel him try to pull away, but she held her ground, her stare boring deep into his.

She pushed against the flow of thought, seeking entrance to his mind. She felt the usual resistance and eased her advance. She was anxious for the connection. She wanted him to know without a doubt that she had all the power now. Pushing against the human mind was like walking against the tide. It could be done, but you needed to place each step carefully. The human mind was fragile. Not that he needed to be sane to be useful, but she wanted him to know the full truth, to feel as inferior as he had tried to make everyone else feel.

The tendrils of her psyche inched through the barrier. His brain yielded to her insistence and the connection was established. The trace of feathers being drawn across skin filled her mind, and a shudder passed through her body.

Her mind jerked, started to pull out. The touch of the mind to her was as physical as holding hands. She started, took a breath, and counted to three. Her fingers tapped a rhythm on the wall where she'd braced herself. She could just tell him, but this was the ultimate domination. Over him, as well as herself.

"Your planet is fairly unstable. The major earthquakes are good for us, but there are other events as well. Do you recall the 2006 shipwreck in Egypt where a thousand people were lost? The Titanic was a good one too." She spoke directly to his mind, ensuring he understood her superiority.

Judi watched C.J.'s response through his own inner eye. She flooded his mind with snippets of news footage from natural disasters. She saw the disconnected scenes she fed him and waited while his human brain pieced together what she was saying. Slowly the puzzle in his mind resolved into a clear picture.

She reluctantly drew back, letting the link slip away. It was never good to keep the connection open too long. She had been told that once the shock wore off, one of them might figure out how to use it. She hadn't really believed it, but why take the chance?

Her touching him was bad enough. If his mind reached out to hers, she didn't think she could keep her composure. She twitched at the thought, stepping back and settling onto the couch again to keep her knees from giving way. At least she was still in control of herself, although her skin crawled and her mind tingled. She'd need a good shower and some mental cleansing exercises later.

"Our best attempt was during your Second World War."

He coughed on the sip of whiskey he had managed to take. Judi grinned. She was enjoying this.

"Oh yes, Hitler was one of us. Pete actually. We still catch him speaking German from time to time."

"But … But why?" His gaze switched from her to the darkening expanse of space outside the ship.

"It's no real secret." She shifted slightly, smoothed her skirt, and waited for him to meet her gaze. "We're hungry."

Contributors

Luka Dowell is a second-year literature major at the University of California, Santa Cruz. He is one of four members of the school's College Unions Poetry Slam Invitational (CUPSI) team and a well respected poet in the local community. They are an open advocate for feminism, transgender representation, minority rights, and leftist ideology; their writing often encourages social and political awareness. He teaches academic essay composition and sells on-the-spot poetry commissions in downtown Santa Cruz.

Heather Dubois is a short story author. She is a member of the Inlandia Institute and has work appearing in the Inlandia Creative Writing Annual Anthology. When she's not working on new short stories or her novel, she's moonlighting as an environmental consultant, trying out new story ideas on her husband and toddler, and wrangling her menagerie of dogs, cats, and tortoise.

Lynn Finger has been an avid writer all her life, self-publishing at a young age. Her first story at age 8 years, was, "Billy and the Dragon," and she has shown a preference for fantasy and sci-fi ever since. Lynn likes to write stories that explore the interface between humans and machines in futuristic worlds. Her family has an informal book club, and the most recent sci fi they read was "Ready Player One." Recently Lynn has published a series of futuristic stories featuring Sofia Goodrek through Elm Books. Lynn grew up in Southern California, and currently lives in Arizona.

Yvette Franklin is a beach loving, LA living, cancer surviving writer and editor. She has greatly appreciated her time hanging with the Deaf and Disability communities over many many years.

Leslie Kung was born in the 80's, a child of immigrants. She survived speech delay as a child, Sensory Integration Disorder, the Chicago public school system, growing up Asian in America, the upheaval and reinvention of college (earning a dual bachelor's of English and Philosophy), the traumatic birth of her first child, domestic violence and PTSD. She writes a variety of fiction, all enriched with cultural, social and experiential depth drawn from lived experience. She resides in Iowa with three small humans, two leopard geckos, and a mysteriously self-sustaining tank of guppies.

David Preyde is a freelance writer who writes about the difficulties of being human. His pieces often explore topics related to disability justice, autism, relationships, and sexuality. David writes creative fiction and non-fiction pieces including a recent coming-of-age novel about a year in the life of a boy with undiagnosed Asperger's Syndrome and a self-help guide about surviving high school as a teenager on the spectrum. He is also an emerging playwright and produces plays that challenge notions of normality and convention. His blog is www.differentsortofsolitude@wordpress.com.

When he was 12 years old, **Colin Stricklin** wrote a fan letter to Ray Bradbury. The response was hand-written: "Dear Colin: I was 12 when I started to write! Write every day, every day, every day!" That letter is now framed and hanging above Stricklin's writing desk. He tries to follow its advice. Colin is, in no particular order, a Wyomingite, planeswalker, Ithaca College grad, novelist, arts advocate, fauchard enthusiast, husband, and Game Master.

Most of what you need to know about Editor **Leonie Skye** and what she likes can be reduced to three moments in her life: 1) That time the light fell green in Koto-In temple in Kyoto and the rain came down in buckets as she sipped hot matcha and watched the moss grow from a covered porch. 2) The moment she realized she was in love while flying over the interchange from the 10 East to the 405 North and suddenly felt like she was really flying. 3) The moment she looked into her daughter's angry newborn eyes and realized she was made of moonlight. She likes when ordinary life gets magical out of nowhere. She lives in Los Angeles. But you can find her on Facebook or on Twitter as @leonie_skye.

Want more from Elm Books?

Check out our website at www.elm-books.com.

You can find our short story anthologies in paperback and on Kindle. Looking for mysteries? Try *Undeath and the Detective*, *Death on a Cold Night*, *Death and the Detective*, or *Death and a Cup of Tea* – or get the last three together for Kindle in *Death in a Box*. Make sure not to miss our romance collections: the fantastical *Fae Love* and the festive *Christmas is for Bad Girls*. And stay tuned for *Light Space*, the sequel collection to *Dark Space*.

Interested in becoming an Elm Books author? You can always find our current calls for submissions on our website.

If you enjoyed this collection, sign up for our mailing list at eepurl.com/bTXa2f. and like us on Facebook at www.facebook.com/ElmBooks! You'll never miss an update on our sales, coupons, and future calls for submissions. We'd love to stay in touch!

$14\underline{95}$

New

CPSIA information can be obtained
at www.ICGtesting.com
Printed in the USA
BVHW04s2056140718
521639BV00024B/502/P